She was the first woman he'd allowed so close.

Two years he had worked to seduce her, drawing her ever closer. At first, it was nothing more than a positioning strategy. Her coffee shop was located directly across the street from the Colby Agency. As time passed, he'd found himself noticing things about her. Like her smile. He missed her when they were apart. That confession rattled him. How had this happened? He'd been taught from birth not to feel any emotion. With Maggie he'd been too human, too weak to resist her, and that had put her in danger.

Now there was only one thing to do.

With one last look at her he walked out the door, the backpack on one shoulder, the automatic in his waistband. He pushed all other thoughts from his mind except the mission.

He would never be safe until the job was done. And neither would Maggie.

DEBRA WEBB

DECODED

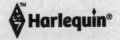

Harlequin®

TORONTO NEW YORK LONDON
AMSTERDAM PARIS SYDNEY HAMBURG
STOCKHOLM ATHENS TOKYO MILAN MADRID
PRAGUE WARSAW BUDAPEST AUCKLAND

First, I must thank friend and awesome Colby fan Patsy Adkins or helping me
make a big choice for the Colby family in this story. You are awesome, Patsy!

Decoded is dedicated to one woman in particular, Aliya, but also to a group of
wonderful people who give selflessly to NGOs (non-government organizations)
all over the world. Aliya and her team have traveled far and wide to selflessly
help the victims of devastation. Just this year, 2011, they traveled to Japan to help
with the horrific tragedy there.
Thank you, Aliya, for your compassion and for the courage to act.

ISBN-13: 978-0-373-69580-5

DECODED

Copyright © 2011 by Debra Webb

Recycling programs
for this product may
not exist in your area.

ABOUT THE AUTHOR

Debra Webb wrote her first story at age nine and her first romance at thirteen. It wasn't until she spent three years working for the military behind the Iron Curtain and within the confining political walls of Berlin, Germany, that she realized her true calling. A five-year stint with NASA on the space shuttle program reinforced her love of the endless possibilities within her grasp as a storyteller. A collision course between suspense and romance was set. Debra has been writing romantic suspense and action-packed romantic thrillers since. Visit her at www.DebraWebb.com or write to her at P.O. Box 4889, Huntsville, AL 35815.

Books by Debra Webb

HARLEQUIN INTRIGUE

*Colby Agency
‡The Equalizers
‡‡Colby Agency: Elite Reconnaissance Division
**Colby Agency: Under Siege
†††Colby Agency: Merger
‡‡‡Colby Agency: Christmas Miracles
†Colby Agency: The New Equalizers
††Colby Agency: Secrets

CAST OF CHARACTERS

Slade Keaton—He is the enigmatic head of the Equalizers, a private investigations firm that ensures justice outside the law as often as inside. Keaton has secrets that even the woman who loves him is afraid to uncover. Those secrets involve the Colby Agency, and now a dangerous enemy has been roused. Keaton must stop the Dragon before she destroys the people he has come to care about. Can he hope to survive?

Maggie James—She has suspected for a while that Slade Keaton is not who and what he seems, but she is desperately in love with him. Still, Maggie is no fool. She has to do the right thing… but what about the baby she is carrying?

Lucas Camp—Lucas fears that Slade Keaton represents a serious threat to his wife, Victoria, and to him. But is Lucas ready for the truth Keaton's real story will reveal? Whether he is ready or not, the past has crashed into the present and Lucas must face his most vicious enemy to date.

Victoria Colby-Camp—Victoria will fight for those she loves. Her compassion for Slade Keaton may very well save his life.

Alayna—Alayna has been a loyal subject to the Dragon. But can she look the other way when her brother's life is threatened? Or will she finally stand up to the monster who is her mother?

Dragon—Pure evil. She might be nothing more than a legend or myth in the Intelligence world. But Lucas Camp and Slade Keaton know just how real and dangerous she is. She has awakened and is poised to devour anyone who gets in the way of her destroying Slade Keaton.

Jim Colby—He is the son of Victoria Colby-Camp, head of the Colby Agency. He has had his reservations about Slade Keaton, however no one understands secrets better than Jim. First and foremost, Jim will protect his mother. But part of him needs to reach out to Keaton, a man who is in the middle of a horrendous nightmare that is all too familiar to Jim Colby.

Ian Michaels and Simon Ruhl—Victoria's most trusted colleagues. These two men serve as seconds-in-command at the Colby Agency.

Chapter One

Maggie James parked her car two blocks beyond the brownstone where *he* would be. She shut off the lights and engine and sat in the darkness. He hadn't stopped by the coffee shop tonight the way he always did. The way he had done for two years.

Emotion burned Maggie's eyes. *Two years.* How had she allowed this to happen? It wasn't enough that she had been a fool. She had known their relationship was make-believe. That he was a fantasy. Not a single thing he had told her would be the truth. Not his name, not the vague past he'd tossed to her like a bone for a starving dog.

Nothing.

Everything about him was a carefully planned deception. Every fiber of her being sensed the duplicity and yet she couldn't point to one instance where he had contradicted himself. There hadn't been a single trip up, but she knew. She just knew.

If she'd had a lick of gumption she should have walked away long ago. Her instincts had warned her time and time again. *He's dangerous. This isn't real.*

But she hadn't listened. Maggie Sue James, thirty-two years old, had pretended it didn't matter. Each time she had worked up the nerve to tell him to stay away, he'd walked into her coffee shop and she'd lost her courage in that same second. Her knees had gone rubbery and her heart had overridden her brain. He had taken control of her as easily and completely as if she had been a mere puppet.

Maggie swallowed back the lump in her throat. She was addicted to him. There was no denying the truth. Sleep eluded her if he wasn't in her bed. Her very soul ached if more than a day passed without him making love to her. Even though the intensity of his lovemaking terrified her at times, she could not resist. How was that possible? No man, not even her low-life former husband, had held that kind of power over her. She'd been a lot younger back then. Wasn't she supposed to be smarter now?

But everything had changed for Maggie sixteen hours and twenty minutes ago. That defining instant had somehow cleared the fog from her brain, and her entire life had zoomed into vivid focus.

At 7:40 a.m. she had finally summoned the courage to take a pregnancy test. It had been positive. *Positive.*

She was pregnant and plenty old enough to know better. How had this happened? She swallowed those little daily pills faithfully. Never missed a day. Ever. Two more tests an hour or so later—long enough to frantically dash to the corner drugstore—had both confirmed the same reality. Maggie was pregnant.

Squaring her shoulders, she pushed aside the apron she'd shed once she'd gotten into the car, and grabbed her purse. A busy night at the coffee shop had distracted her from this necessary business for a while. At closing time the anger had started to build once more, pounding in her skull like the threatening winds of a hurricane. The next thing she knew, she had been in her car headed here. This couldn't wait any longer.

Over the past eight years she had climbed a couple of mountains. She had finally dumped her no-good, cheating husband. The move from Indianapolis to Chicago had given her a fresh start. Two years later she'd bought the drowning coffee shop and she'd turned it into the place to stop while shopping or working on the Magnificent Mile. Her name had become the talk around watercoolers and in checkout lines. She had worked hard to achieve that success—and she'd done it during the worst of the sluggish economy.

She could do this. Slade Keaton wasn't interested in a wife, much less a child. He would be glad to let her go just as soon as she informed him that she was pregnant. Anger elbowed aside the softer emotions. Oh, he would be only too happy to disappear from her life then. Whatever his reason for hanging around this long, it wasn't about her. That made for a bad relationship regardless of the other concerns she suspected.

Well, that was fine. Maggie opened her car door and climbed out. The late-autumn chill invaded her jacket, making her shiver. The sooner he was out of her life for good, the better off she would be. Maybe then she could finally move on.

Maggie surveyed the street in both directions before locking her car. This wasn't exactly a bad neighborhood anymore, but at night there was no such thing as a really good neighborhood. The row of brownstones lined two blocks. Some were still private residences, but most had been turned into businesses years ago.

Her hands burrowed deep into her pockets, cell phone clasped in her right, as she walked toward the brownstone on the end of the first block. The windows were dark. Her steps slowed. He had to be here. When he wasn't at her small apartment over the coffee shop, he was here, at his place of business on the ground floor, or in his second-floor apartment.

Maggie scanned the vehicles parked along the street. His sedan wasn't among them. There was an alley along the rear of the row of brownstones. During the daylight hours city maintenance and garbage collection vehicles required full access, but at night the area was fair game. Maybe he'd parked there. Maybe he'd called it a night, which would explain the lack of lights.

And maybe she was crazy for coming here at this hour. Then again, he'd left her little choice when he didn't show at the coffee shop. She had to do this while she still had the nerve. The needling notion that something was wrong cut through all the confusion in her brain, leaking a new kind of fear into her belly. He'd always come to watch the folks at the Colby Agency leave for the night. Never failed.

But not tonight.

What if he'd already left? Just walked away? Running his private-investigations firm from some other location was certainly possible. Slade didn't do any of the actual investigating himself. He rarely met with clients.

He could be gone.

Her knees felt a little wobbly and her stomach churned with uncertainty. Wouldn't that be a good thing? She wanted him out of her life. He wouldn't be interested in a child. Why tell him? Leaving out that complication would make this entire matter far simpler. The last thing she wanted was for him to hang around just for the sake of the child. What kind of father would he make if forced into the role?

What kind of mother would she make?

Dear God, what am I going to do? Terror nipped at her. She wrenched her hands from her pockets and wrapped her arms around her waist. She'd always taken care of herself, yes. But this was a child! A whole human life that would be counting on her! What if she screwed up? What if she couldn't do it? Her parents had been hardworking, salt-of-the-earth people. Good parents. Would she be a good mother? And could she assume the part of father, as well?

Her younger sister had three kids, but she also had a husband who was a fantastic dad. Heck, her older sister had five kids and she'd done just fine after her husband died.

Maggie kicked aside the fears and doubts and grabbed back her courage. She was a James. Having a houseful of kids was the norm. Truth was, Maggie had wanted kids a long time ago, but her bum of a husband had put off the idea. Lucky for Maggie and the prospective children.

Sadly, the only thing thoughts of her ex proved was that Maggie was foolish enough to fall hard for the wrong kind of guy twice.

When would she learn?

A little late to worry about that now.

Her cell vibrated. Maggie dragged it from her pocket

and stared at the screen. It was *him*. Her heart commenced that crazy gallop.

She considered not answering. But wasn't talking to him why she was here? He could be waiting for her back at her place.

Maggie cleared her throat. "Hello." She struggled to slow her breathing and tune out the pounding in her ears. *Be calm. Stay focused.* This was far too important to allow emotions to override her good sense.

"Turn around and walk back to your car."

A trickle of fresh fear seeped into her chest. "What?" Maggie glanced around. "Where are you?"

"Walk back to your car. Now."

She swiped a wisp of hair from her cheek. "Not until you tell me where you are." She was finished. No more games. No more fantasies. This was reality. Butterflies swirled in her stomach.

"This is not the time to turn stubborn, Maggie." His voice was stern, just shy of harsh.

Frustration tightened her lips. She shoved the phone back into her pocket. She wanted to just keep walking in the other direction. Actually what she wanted to do was call him back and tell him to go to hell.

Instead, she obeyed like a submissive child.

You can't keep doing this, Maggie!

She was a grown woman. With a child on the way! She had to get past this. Do a 12-step program. Something. Slade Keaton was trouble and she needed him out of her life. Now.

Her lips trembled. Tears brimmed on her lashes. *Idiot. Idiot.* She stamped the rest of the way back to her car, hit the remote unlock and got behind the wheel.

"Now what?" she muttered to herself. Was this a

game to him? This was her life and she was sick of games. She should just leave and never look back.

Where the hell was he? Her car's interior lamp faded to black. Obviously he could see her from wherever he was. *Coward.*

"Start the engine and drive away."

Her breath caught. Their gazes locked in the rearview mirror. How had he gotten into her car? Hadn't she locked it? She'd hit the unlock on the remote two steps before reaching the car, which was habit, but there wouldn't have been a warning that the doors were unlocked already. Where was her brain?

"Hurry, Maggie. I don't know how much time we have left."

Her hand shook as she picked through the keys for the right one. All the questions she wanted to hurl at him clogged into a huge knot in her throat, and the thick silence throbbing inside the car made it hard to breathe. It took two attempts to get the key into the ignition. A quick twist and the engine started.

"Drive."

The tone of that one word warned her that she shouldn't ask any questions. She set the headlamps to the on position and eased away from the curb.

"Where are we going?" She hated that her voice trembled. Damn him.

"Just drive."

Fury blasted her. That was it. She'd had enough. Maggie slammed her foot on the brake. The car rocked to a stop. "Where are we going?" She was a grown woman. She had responsibilities, first and foremost to herself.

"Maggie."

She closed her eyes, couldn't bear to hear him say her name. "Stop. Just stop." She shook her head. "I can't do this anymore."

"We have to move," he urged. "We can talk later. Right now you just have to trust me."

Maggie laughed. She didn't mean to, but the sound, brittle and painful, just burst out of her. "You have to be kidding!" She was hysterical. The stress had evidently pushed her over the edge.

When cold steel pressed against her temple, her attention swung to the rearview mirror. He had a gun to her head. A gun! "What're you doing?"

"Drive, Maggie. Just drive."

Her fingers tightened around the steering wheel. Forcing her foot to move from the brake to the accelerator, she reminded herself to breathe. She'd made a terrible, terrible mistake.

An explosion fragmented the silence. Light burst to her left, changing the darkness to a brilliant yellow. Pieces of something showered down on her car. Not hail…but rocks or pieces of brick.

As if in slow motion, she turned to stare out the car window. The brownstone where Slade worked and lived had blown up. Flames licked toward the stars. Pieces of the building lay on the sidewalk…on the street. On the hood of her car.

"Go, Maggie! Hurry!"

Somehow her foot punched the accelerator. The car lunged forward.

She tried to blink away the images, her fingers cramped from clutching the steering wheel so tightly. This couldn't be happening. The man she loved—the father of her unborn child—had put a gun to her head. His office—his apartment—had just exploded.

In that moment her reality sharpened into perfect clarity. She had never known this man. She had suspected as much. Her intuition had warned repeatedly that he was hiding something. Everything. Above all else, his identity.

Maggie slammed on the brakes, harder this time. She glared at his reflection in the rearview mirror. "Who are you?"

He leaned forward, reached up and threaded his fingers into her hair. His hold tightened as he pulled her closer. She should scream. She knew this. But his slightest touch rendered her totally helpless.

"I know you better than you know yourself, Maggie. I know you want to trust me."

She wanted to argue. The words refused to form on her tongue. The sound of his voice slid around her, tethering her as surely as if he'd used steel bands. How could she lose all control so easily? Where was her courage? Her logic?

His lips pressed nearer to her ear. She shivered. "If you don't do as I say we're both going to die. I, for one, have no desire to die tonight."

The cold steel of the weapon he held snuggled against her throat. "Now, drive."

Chapter Two

Victoria Colby-Camp heard the ring of the bedside phone, but the concept of opening her eyes and answering was far too difficult to grasp. The sound of her husband's voice as he took the call parted the constricting layers of sleep, allowing her to rouse more fully. Who would call at this hour?

"Was anyone hurt?"

Victoria sat up, instantly wide awake. "What's happened?" Was it Jim or one of the children? A member of their extended family at the Colby Agency? Fear roared through her body like a fire set to dry kindling.

"We'll be right there." Lucas heaved a weary breath as he placed the phone back into its cradle and turned to his wife. "A friend from Chicago P.D. called Jim. We don't have any real details just yet, but there's been an explosion at the brownstone."

The offices of Jim's old firm, the Equalizers. Almost two years ago now, Slade Keaton had taken over the firm since Jim had joined Victoria at the Colby Agency. Early last year Keaton had moved into the renovated upstairs apartment of the brownstone. Jim had gone there shortly after midnight to confront him regarding their suspicions as to his true identity. He'd found no sign of Keaton. Thank God Jim hadn't been in or near the building when the explosion occurred.

"Was anyone in the building?" Maggie James, the owner of the coffee shop across the street from the Colby Agency offices, was Keaton's girlfriend. Anguish tore through Victoria. She prayed they were both safe. Whoever Keaton was and whatever he had done, Victoria wished him no harm. And Maggie was innocent in all this. Her only misstep was falling in love with a man whose past was an enigma that even Lucas hadn't been able to decipher.

"The explosion occurred less than an hour ago. Maybe fifteen minutes after Jim was there looking for Keaton." Lucas adjusted his prosthetic leg and stood. "They've only just gotten the fire under control. They're waiting for the rubble to cool to start the search."

Victoria dropped her feet to the carpeted floor and rushed to the closet for clothes. "Were any of the neighboring buildings damaged?" she called out to Lucas. The brownstones along the two nearly identical blocks were structurally connected. She doubted one could have been destroyed without damage to one or more of the others. Since most were businesses, she prayed no one had been working late. The injury or death of the innocent was always the most devastating in deliberate acts such as this. Admittedly, she had no way of knowing if the explosion was deliberate just yet. However, based on the events that had taken place recently related to Keaton, she felt confident that the explosion was the result of foul play.

"The two buildings on either side were damaged,

but Jim didn't mention to what extent. He may not have known. He's en route. We'll be right behind him. Perhaps there will be more information by then."

Victoria dressed and stepped into a pair of comfortable leather slides, not bothering with socks. Grabbing a clasp from her bedside table, she tucked up her shoulder-length hair. Lucas was dressed in jeans and a sweatshirt and sneakers, no less. She so rarely saw him dressed casually that she almost smiled in spite of the circumstances. Thank God for him. As much as she loved her son and her grandchildren, her life would not be complete without Lucas.

Victoria grabbed her purse as they hurried to the garage. Lucas tucked his weapon into the waistband of his jeans. Ever the gentleman, he opened then closed her car door before climbing behind the wheel. As soon as they backed out into the driveway, the house and garage were secured with a single click of the security remote. The rest of their small gated community was tucked in for the night. The gas streetlamps and lovely landscape lighting had a calming effect. As scary as the world could be sometimes, she was very thankful for a safe and pleasant neighborhood.

With her nerves settled, Victoria used the time as Lucas drove through the darkness to consider the possible causes of the explosion. Gas leak…? Explosive device? Did Keaton keep explosives on hand? Surely that was not the case.

Considering what had happened only days ago to Levi Stark and Casey Manning, Lucas's goddaughter, in Acapulco, Keaton had made some powerful enemies. Had those enemies caught up with him this night?

Victoria blinked away the images that immediately

attempted to intrude. She didn't want to think about the woman…the one they called the Dragon. According to Levi and Casey, she looked a great deal like Victoria— like a sister. That Lucas had had an affair with the woman made it hard for Victoria to breathe.

But that was in the past. Thirty years ago. Victoria had no right to feel jealousy about that time. If this woman was Keaton's mother, as suggested from the results of Levi and Casey's investigation, she clearly had no motherly feelings for her son. That part of the intelligence—the biological connection—had not been corroborated, so it was best not to speculate. Bottom line, the Dragon was an enemy to Keaton and, it seemed, to Lucas.

The idea made no sense. Why wait all these years to strike? Of course, she may have only just located Keaton. Perhaps thanks to Victoria and Lucas trolling his history. As much as she wanted the truth in order to assess any threat from Keaton, Victoria genuinely hoped she and Lucas had not triggered this tragedy.

"This has nothing to do with anything you did."

Her husband had read her mind. The tension banded around her chest eased the slightest bit. "How can you be so sure?" She had sent Levi down to Mexico. Keaton had stirred her suspicions and she'd reacted. Dear God, what had they done?

"This one is on me," Lucas said quietly. "You need to understand that. You have no part in that world."

The question Victoria had wanted to ask for the past twenty-four hours pressed against her skull. She needed to know. But did she have a right to know? "Are you certain I had no part in what happened?" She held her breath. The woman looked like Victoria, after all. Had that been the reason Lucas had turned to her all those years ago?

Two, then three beats of silence passed. Lucas reached for her hand. "Let's not do this to ourselves until we have the facts. Whatever is happening may be about Keaton only. The ordeal in Mexico may have been a way to smoke him out once our connection to him was established." Lucas exhaled a big breath. "The fact is, we can't rule out or confirm anything yet."

Victoria ordered herself to breathe. Lucas had assumed her question was about the current situation. In time they would need to talk about her other question, the one she really needed to ask. But that would have to wait.

This puzzle had to be pieced together very carefully, one fragment at a time. Far too much was at stake to go about this any other way.

THE BROWNSTONE STILL smoldered when they arrived on the block. Jim waited for them just outside the perimeter of the crime scene. The cold filtered right through the thick sweater Victoria had chosen. She hugged her arms around herself and hoped for good news about Keaton and Maggie.

"Still no word on victims," Jim said as they approached. "I called Maggie's home number as well as the coffee shop and there's no answer. Keaton isn't answering his cell and his car is parked in the alley." Jim jerked his head toward the brownstone. "It'll be hours before we know the probable cause of the explosion and if there are victims."

The chill invading her bones turned Victoria's blood to ice. "What about the neighboring buildings?"

"One's empty and the other's a business. The owner has confirmed that no one employed there was in the building tonight."

Thank God for that news. Victoria stared at the wreck that had been the home of the Equalizers. Her instincts warned that this was deliberate, calculated destruction. Whoever had done this either wanted Keaton dead or wanted to send him a very loud message.

Lucas and Jim discussed the steps that would be taken by the police and fire departments. Victoria tried to pay attention, but her mind kept wandering to Maggie and how all this would affect her—if she was still alive. Dread ached in Victoria's bones.

Jim had tried to reach Keaton all night, but he'd simply disappeared. Victoria had considered calling Maggie or paying her a visit to warn her. What would she have said? I think the man you love is dangerous?

Regret settled, heavy and sickening, in Victoria's stomach. She should have warned Maggie.

Now it might be too late.

Chapter Three

2:32 a.m.

Slade Keaton... He didn't know why he continued to consider himself by that name. That life was over. If he'd needed convincing, the past couple of hours had confirmed that fact. Hanging on to such superficial trappings was a grave error. He knew this.

Another change wasn't the end of the world. He'd changed his name so many times during the latter part of his thirty years on this earth that he couldn't even remember all the ones he'd used. This was not a new scenario to him.

Yet, somehow, it felt like the end of the world...like a whole new concept. Because of her. His gaze settled on the woman behind the wheel. Slade closed his eyes and shook his head. He'd made a mistake. That, he could say with complete confidence, was a first. He opened his eyes and focused his attention on the dark road ahead. A man like him couldn't afford careless mistakes. He'd been trained better than that.

Images from his formative years attempted to invade his concentration. He kicked them aside. The past was irrelevant. Nothing mattered except today…this moment. He would not die for *her*.

Rage tightened his lips. Mother. *Madre*. The woman who had been anything but a mother to him. He had eluded her, just as he had eluded the rest of the world, for a dozen years now. No one had cornered him. But his recent mistake had allowed her to find him. Now there was only one way this could end.

One of them had to die.

The idea of killing his own mother evoked only one emotion. *Determination*.

"What now?"

Slade shifted his attention back to the here and now. Maggie had stopped at an intersection. Deep, dark woods closed in on all sides, leaving the highway nothing but a black river flowing in front of the headlights. Even the moon and stars had concealed themselves as if they, too, sensed the impending doom.

"Do I go straight or turn?" Her voice was sharp but still shaky. She was scared and rightly so. Maggie James had no idea how close to death she'd already come. If he was successful in maintaining her cooperation, she would never know.

"Take a right." Slade calculated the miles before they reached the motel. Four, maybe five more. The place was a dump, but it was close to the interstate and there was a café next door. It would fulfill his immediate requirements.

Maggie made the turn and drove onward through the darkness. She'd stopped asking questions an hour ago. Mostly because of the weapon he'd wielded. Guilt nudged him. He'd done what he had to. She might never realize it, but he'd saved her life.

"How much farther?"

It looked as if she was through with the silent treatment. "Not far now." She wasn't going to like the next step in his plan any more than she'd liked the last. There was nothing he could do about that. Time was of the essence.

The headlamps spotlighted a road sign in the distance indicating a ramp to the interstate. After he'd covered arrangements for Maggie, he'd take that interstate to St. Louis. From there he had private air transport to Mexico City. He had contacts in Mexico City. This war would require extensive resources. And a whole lot of something he'd been short on his whole life—good luck.

Luck, right. He had made his own way in this life. Depending on luck would have offered him as much security as counting on his so-called mother to be a parent. Not happening.

Slade hadn't actually missed having a real parent. One couldn't miss what one hadn't had. But, recently, he had begun to wonder what it would have felt like. What his life would have been like had his circumstances been different. How would it feel to have a real relationship?

He was a fool. Fury hardened his jaw. He should not have stayed in Chicago so long. Weakness had invaded, making him soft and stupid. He would never have a real anything. He was not real, not in that sense.

The motel's aged neon sign strained upward, high above the one-story queue of run-down rooms, in order to be seen by travelers on the interstate. Two tractor-trailers were parked along the side of the road. There wouldn't be enough space on the old strip of a parking lot for rigs that size, but the motel offered drivers a cheap place to sleep for a few hours before hitting the road again. Slade had checked out the motel and gotten a profile on the typical guest.

"Pull into the motel parking lot," he instructed, then waited for her to comply. "Park in front of the office."

He'd rented the car under an alias and stashed it for this leg of his departure. He hadn't known then that he would have a passenger. To some degree the snag could work in his favor. Having dumped Maggie's car at the bus station would serve as a ruse, helping to buy sufficient time to get to St. Louis.

Maggie shut off the headlights and the engine. Her hands continued to clutch the steering wheel. Her respiration was slow enough to indicate some level of calmness, but he couldn't be certain of how she would react during the next few minutes.

"We're going in to rent a room." He leaned forward. "Don't force me to do something you'll regret."

"Like you haven't already?"

Her voice didn't wobble now; rather, she sounded weary and resigned and just a little frustrated. That shouldn't make his gut tighten with regret, but it did. He mentally narrowed the situation into focus and blocked those senseless, dangerous emotions. "You'll thank me later. Now, get out."

They emerged simultaneously. He tucked the weapon into his waistband beneath his jacket. His arm went around her waist and she tensed.

"Relax." He paused and looked directly into her green eyes. They glistened with the fear she worked so hard to hide. "We need this to look natural. No trouble, okay?"

She nodded. He gave her a quick kiss on the lips.

Her breath caught and she trembled. The satisfaction he should have felt at having that much power over her failed to make an appearance.

Keeping one arm around her, Slade pushed open the door to the office. A bell jingled. The guy behind the desk looked up from the compact television blaring with the canned laughter of a sitcom. He studied Slade from behind his nerdy eyeglasses. Looked young enough to be a college student or maybe a dropout. Working the graveyard shift apparently made him a little jumpy. He lowered the volume on the set.

"You need a room for the night—" the guy glanced at Maggie "—or the hour?"

Slade didn't smile. He reached into the pocket of his jeans and pulled out a bill big enough to get the clever guy's attention. "The night. We've still got a long way to drive." He pulled Maggie closer and gave her the smile he'd kept from the clerk. "Don't we, baby?"

She nodded, the move jerky. "We… Yes."

The clerk reached for the old-fashioned row of boxes that held actual keys to the available rooms. "Make it on the west end," Slade prompted. "I don't want to wake up with the sun in my eyes."

The clerk tossed a key onto the counter. "Clean sheets are over there." He pointed to a row of shelves on the other side of the room. "Checkout time's 10:00 a.m."

"Thanks." Slade picked up the key, then, keeping Maggie close, grabbed a stack of bed linens.

Outside, Slade opened the passenger-side door of the rental. "Hop in. We'll park in front of the room."

Maggie climbed in and Slade closed her door. He kept an eye on her as he rounded the hood. Those Irish genes of hers could kick in anytime now. Maintaining control was essential.

The view of their room and the sedan would be blocked by the tractor-trailers parked along the road at that end of the property. Any additional layers of security were welcome.

Once parked, Slade was out of the car first and at her side by the time she opened her door. He passed the linens to her, then ushered her to the trunk where he grabbed the one bag he'd brought along, a backpack. To her credit, she didn't scream or try to run or even argue with him as he guided her to the room. She waited quietly as he unlocked the door and opened it. Just as quietly, she walked inside and turned on the lamp on the bedside table. The linens landed in a heap on the naked mattress.

The bare bulb glowing above their door was the only exterior light working on that end of the row of rooms. He unscrewed the bulb and took a final look around the parking lot. They seemed to be in the clear for now.

With the door secured, he checked the bathroom and closet, then placed his bag on the floor and shoved the key into his jacket pocket alongside her cell phone. He'd taken it as soon as they were far enough away from the explosion for her to work up the courage to try to use it without him noticing. He'd turned it off and removed the battery, just in case.

Maggie was strong and brave. He'd admired that about her for the past two years. She would need all the strength and bravery she possessed for what was to come.

As if that courage had abruptly kicked in to full throttle, she turned on him, green eyes blazing as hotly as that mane of red hair. "What kind of trouble are you in—" her lips tightened "—whoever you are?"

"Sit." He gestured to the bed.

Her arms crossed over her chest. "I'm not taking any more orders until you answer my questions."

Weariness hit him hard. Or maybe it was the drain of having her look at him that way. Funny, his entire life he'd never cared what anyone thought of him. He'd stopped caring about that kind of thing by the time he was seven. By twelve he would have killed anyone who got in his way like this. That he tolerated it now startled him still. His indulgence of this unfamiliar aspect of human bonding the past two years was the biggest surprise of all. He'd spent endless hours making this lonely, hardworking woman want him as she had never wanted anyone before. After that, he'd told himself that stringing her along was necessary for his cover.

As it turned out, he had been the fool.

He contemplated drawing his weapon to gain her cooperation, but he lacked sufficient motivation. Instead, he dropped into the chair by the window. The room was a little cold, so he turned on the heat. The box beneath the window rumbled then shook with the effort of noisily blowing out stale air.

"I mean it," she warned when he turned his attention to her once more. "If you don't tell me what's going on, I'm walking out that door."

He dropped his head back on the chair and deliberated as to which lie to offer. There were so many. So many, in fact, that he had to think hard to sift out the most recent ones. Counting the water stains on the ceiling distracted him for a moment. The stains were dark and without uniformity or pattern. Like his life.

As good as her word, Maggie started for the door. He grabbed her arm as she passed his chair. Her gaze collided with his. She was just mad enough to call his bluff. Another funny thing. He never bluffed.

His lapse into the mundane was going to get him killed. And anyone else who had the misfortune of being with or connected to him.

"Maggie, sit down."

She stared at him for an endless moment before relenting. With a frustrated about-face she stamped to the bed and sat, arms still crossed, one foot patting against the ragged, once-beige carpet.

With a heavy breath he settled his eyes on hers. "The people who hit the brownstone—"

"You mean the ones who blew it up?" she snapped. "That's what they did, Slade. They blew it up." She gestured in frustration. "Innocent people may have been injured or killed."

He reached for patience. "No one was injured or killed."

"How do you know?" She shot to her feet. "You can't know!"

"I have a contact who's keeping me informed." He'd received two messages since they left Chicago. Unless an unauthorized person had been inside the buildings on either side of the brownstone that housed the Equalizer offices, no one had been hurt.

Maggie dropped back down to the mattress. "That's one good thing."

He had her attention, so he might as well get to the point. "I need you to stay here for a few days." Her eyes grew rounder with each word he said. "Until the dust settles. When it's safe for you to go home, I'll give you the all clear."

MAGGIE TOOK A MOMENT TO calm the outrage and indignation mounting inside her. She had decided that he had no intention of killing her or he surely would have by now. Still, pushing the issue wouldn't be smart. God knew, she'd been wrong about him all this time, so what made her think she knew anything now?

"Where are you going?" Someone obviously wanted him dead. Was he going to go up against whoever this was alone? She tried her best to ignore the weight on her chest. Why did she care? If she were smart she would let him go and then get out of here as fast as possible. "Who did this? What do they want?"

He braced his forearms on his spread thighs. His unusually dark gray eyes studied hers. "The person responsible for what you witnessed tonight has been looking for me for a very long time. I can't evade her any longer. When this—"

"Her?" Maggie felt her brow furrow in confusion. The person responsible for this insanity was a woman? An old lover? Jealousy flooded her, washing away the harsher emotions she'd hoped to hang on to.

"The less you know," he advised in that deep voice that curled around her like a warm, familiar blanket, "the better. You're already a target simply by virtue of the fact that you've been seen with me."

Maggie's head started to spin. She felt sick to her stomach. How had she gotten herself into this? "I don't understand."

"You have to believe me when I say that she will stop at nothing to get to me. Anyone in her path will go down, too. Anyone she believes she can use to get to me will suffer an even worse fate."

Maggie hugged herself more tightly. Her fingernails

bit into her skin despite the sweater she wore. "What kind of person has enemies like that?" She wasn't totally naive. She watched the news. There were bad people out there. All kinds. But was this about drugs? Guns? Stolen goods? Murder? An angry client of his private-investigations business? Or some past business dealings? What?

She held his gaze, her insides raging with an agonizing twist of emotions. This man was the father of her child. Yet she had no idea why someone would want to kill him. She didn't know him at all.

As if sensing her thoughts, he looked away. "The kind of person you don't want to know."

As cold as he'd been from the moment their gazes locked in her rearview mirror, just now she heard something almost like vulnerability in his voice. But that was impossible. Just her imagination. She wanted to hear real emotion and that wasn't going to happen.

"I'd say it's a little late for that." He'd been dragging her heart around for almost two years now. This wasn't the time to suggest she didn't want to know him. He'd stolen that option from her a long time ago.

Slade pushed to his feet. "There's nothing I can do to change that now." He nudged the curtain aside and stared into the night.

"So that's it." She shook her head. "You steal two years of my life and then you tell me there's nothing you can do to make this right." Hysteria had edged into her voice. She forced it back. "What does that make you, Slade?" A *user*, she didn't say. But it was true. He'd used her to get close to Victoria and Lucas. She understood that part now. If her friends at the Colby Agency were in danger it would be her fault. That confounded quaking started deep inside her once more.

He had weaseled his way into her life for a reason. Something that involved the Colby Agency. Maggie had a right to some answers.

"Why the Colby Agency? They're good people. What could they possibly have done to you?"

He turned around, his face a hard mask she couldn't hope to read. "You think you know people, but you don't. Can you really be certain they're good people? Can you? Really?"

"Of course I can," she retorted without hesitation. "It's you I don't know."

"At least we agree on something."

Maggie dared to take two steps toward him. His gaze narrowed. "You made me love you." Her throat tried to close. She fought the aching emotions. "Just so you could do whatever it was you came to Chicago to do."

More of the dingy carpet between them disappeared as he took a step toward her, matching her stance. The air vanished from her lungs. "I didn't do anything you didn't want me to do."

The tremors grew stronger. She struggled to restrain the visible shaking. "You never felt anything for me, did you?" How could she love the wrong man twice in her life? Hadn't she learned anything the first time around? That part hurt the most. Knowing that she loved him so much and he felt nothing at all.

"Listen to me carefully, Maggie."

He touched her. She couldn't bear it. She drew away.

His hand dropped to his side. "You have one chance at surviving this. If you do exactly as I say, you'll be safe."

As though she would trust anything he said. She laughed. "You said yourself that she'd seen me with you. What's to keep her from coming after me once you're gone?" And what would happen to him? Would he be able to win against this woman who had sought him for so long? Misery writhed inside Maggie. The idea that her child would never know his or her father abruptly tore at her with staggering viciousness.

"I won't let that happen."

How could he make such a promise? "You can't guarantee my safety." If that were the case, they wouldn't be holed up in this hovel. Was he kidding her or himself?

"It's me she wants," he said, his voice weary. "As long as you stay out of the way you'll be safe."

He wasn't going to give her any answers. This man she had come to love was going to leave her and she would never know if he was dead or alive.

"Then go." She pointed to the door. "Just go."

"Don't call anyone you know. Don't leave except to get food from the café next door." He held up his hands for emphasis. "No matter what you hear or see, just stay put until I tell you otherwise."

The pain that coiled inside her as he reached for his bag was very nearly unbearable. How could she just let him go like this? But wasn't that what she wanted? To be free of him? She couldn't trust him. She didn't even know who he was. Her baby would be better off without him. She would be better off.

Then why did it feel as though her world was crashing to an end with every step he took?

He hesitated at the door.

Maggie felt as if her very bones had crumbled, leaving her helpless and unable to move.

Slade turned, his gaze settled on her and he strode back to where she stood. His hand closed around her neck and he pulled her close. He kissed her hard. Made her melt against his body. How could she spend the rest of her life without him?

By the time he drew his lips from hers she was gasping for breath. He pressed his forehead to hers. "You make me wish I was someone else."

He tucked something into her jacket pocket and walked away.

Fiery tears flowed down her cheeks. She would never see him again, never—

The window shattered, raining glass into the room.

Slade spun around, lunged toward her, taking her to the floor and covering her body with his.

"Stay down."

Her heart seized when he scrambled to the bedside table and turned off the lamp. Something thunked against the wall near the bed. Was someone shooting at them? There hadn't been any gunshot blasts.

He moved in close to her in the darkness. "There's a window in the bathroom. You may have to break it to get out."

Was he sending her out the back way alone? Fear crowded into her throat, choking off the air to her lungs. "But what will you—"

"Listen to me, Maggie."

The base of the lamp on the bedside table burst. Maggie screamed.

"I'm going out that door to draw them away. I'll fire three shots in a row when it's clear for you to go out the back. Run as far into the woods as you can and stay there until you hear sirens. The police will come."

Before she could argue, he was opening the door.

A bullet thwacked into the doorjamb just above his head. Fear crammed into her chest.

Maggie struggled with the need to run after him. But she had to protect her baby. She crawled to the bathroom, crept inside and closed the door.

For long seconds or minutes, she couldn't say for sure which, she sat on the floor, her back against the wall, and tried to catch her breath. Her heart pounded so fast it hurt.

She prayed hard for her child's protection. For Slade's protection. She checked her pocket to see what he'd put there, part of her hoping for a note that explained everything. Cash. She closed her eyes and fought the wave of tears.

A sharp sound cut through the silence. Then a second gunshot. A third rang out and her muscles instinctively reacted. She sprang to her feet and felt for the window. It was large enough, but the lower sash didn't want to budge. She double-checked that it was unlocked, then pushed upward with every ounce of strength in her body.

The window slowly slid up.

She listened for a moment, then climbed onto the closed toilet lid and thrust her head out the window. It was dark as pitch behind the motel. Trees crowded close to the back of the building.

Maggie scrambled out, almost falling in her haste. When her feet were firmly on the ground, she steadied herself and started toward the woods.

Another gunshot echoed in the night.

Did that mean Slade was still okay? The other weapons hadn't made that sound.

"Well, well," a male voice—not Slade's—announced from behind her. Something hard nudged her in the back. "Just where do you think you're going?"

A scream withered in her throat.

"That's what I thought," he taunted. "Nowhere. Now, get down on your knees and I'll make this quick."

Maggie had no weapon. She couldn't even seem to scream.

He was going to kill her even if she did exactly as he said.

Maggie ran. She burst forward like a racehorse let loose from the starting gate. The ground seemed to move under her feet even as she leaned forward to advance her escape. Every muscle in her body tensed, waiting for the inevitable burn of hot lead piercing her skin.

A blast ricocheted in her ears.

She stumbled and fell face-first to the ground.

Chapter Four

The air exited Slade's lungs.

The moon peeked from behind the clouds just enough to highlight Maggie's body facedown on the ground. An unfamiliar sensation slammed into his gut. Was she hit?

He was at her side before the question stopped throbbing in his skull.

She grunted and started to push herself up.

The relief that roared through his veins sent a quake along his limbs. He helped her up, tried to see any injury despite the lack of decent light. "Maggie, did you take a hit?"

She pushed the hair out of her face and looked around. Her attention locked on the guy with the bullet in the back of his skull three feet from her and her breath caught. She made a panicked sound and stumbled back, her body trembling in fear.

There was no time for hysteria. Slade shook her even as he gave himself a mental shake. "Maggie, are you injured?"

She moved her head side to side. "No." Her hand went to her stomach. "I'm okay. I think I'm okay."

"We need to hurry." He couldn't wait for her to regain

her equilibrium or take the time to check the dead guy for ID. They had to get out of here.

Maggie held up a hand. "Give me a second." She swayed, took a breath and visibly attempted to steady herself.

Slade gritted his teeth and reached for patience. How the hell had *she* found him so quickly? His contact, no doubt. Bud McCain was the only resource in the States that Slade trusted fully. He'd intervened in Acapulco, ultimately saving the lives of Lucas Camp's goddaughter and Colby Agency investigator Levi Stark. That move, however, had obviously put McCain on the Dragon's radar. She had likely tracked him down and made him pay.

Fury raged in Slade's gut. His best resource and friend, if he'd ever had one, was likely dead. There was no other explanation for *her* learning Slade's plans. McCain would never have given up a single detail, but his cell phone or computer would have cyber tracks of where he'd been and what he'd done. A top-notch analyst would be able to find those tracks no matter how well hidden or how meticulously wiped. She would select only the very best in each field for her elite team. Damn her.

Slade should have killed her when he'd had the chance, but he'd scarcely been more than a kid. What does a child know of right versus wrong, bizarre versus normal?

Pushing aside the pointless obsessing, he quickly ticked off their options. Transportation to St. Louis might very well be compromised. The more immediate problem was getting out of here fast.

Slade swore as sirens wailed in the distance.

The car was out of the question now. The highway, too. The increasingly deafening blare of the approaching police made that all too clear.

Hiking his bag onto his shoulder, Slade surveyed the tree line.

The options were sorely limited. "You ready now?"

Maggie nodded.

Running was better than nothing.

Her hand tight in his, he sprinted into the woods.

MAGGIE STRUGGLED TO KEEP UP. Her chest heaved in desperation, but the air just wouldn't find its way into her lungs. That man was dead...Slade had killed him. But the man had had a gun to her head. Would he have killed her if Slade hadn't stopped him?

Yes.

Of that part she was sure. Sweet Lord, there was no escaping these people.

She couldn't do this.

The police were coming to the motel. She'd heard the sirens. She and Slade should go back, explain the situation and get help. He couldn't do this alone.

Maggie wrenched her hand free of his. The loss of momentum made her stumble. She hit the ground on her hands and knees. Before she could get up and run the other way, Slade was reaching for her.

"We can't go back, Maggie."

The trees blocked any prospect of light. She could make out his form but little else. What difference did it make? No matter how well she knew his eyes...his face...every part of him, she didn't know *him*. The longer she allowed her foolish indecisiveness to drag out, the harder it would be to do the right thing. "I won't

do this." She shook her head. "I can't. I'm going back."
If she did the right thing, maybe he would, too.

Maggie turned around and did what she should have
done hours ago. She walked away from the danger that
was Slade Keaton.

"You have no reason to trust me."

His words shouldn't have stalled her next step, but
they did. Dear God, what was wrong with her? She had
more sense than this under normal circumstances. Had
she lost her mind? She almost laughed out loud. What
kind of question was that? Of course she had lost her
mind!

"But ask yourself this," he went on as the desperate
debate continued inside her.

She didn't want to hear anything he had to say. His
words and the sound of his voice confused her. She tried
to shake him from her head, tried to quiet the questions
and doubts spinning out of control in her brain, but he
just kept talking.

"Why did I bring you with me?"

The sirens were closer now. Just a few yards through
those trees. She stared into the darkness, torn between
running and facing his question.

"You have no negotiation value. You'll only slow me
down."

Maggie closed her eyes and fought back the tears
burning there.

"She has never gotten this close."

Turning slowly to prevent the churning emotions
from throwing her off balance, Maggie confronted him.
"You want me to believe that you're protecting me?"
The notion was completely ridiculous. She wouldn't
even be here if not for him and his secrets that a master

cryptographer couldn't hope to decode. He had barged into her life, thrown out a baited hook and she had swallowed it without once stepping back and considering the consequences. He had consumed her existence, and his presence had put her in danger. How dare he blame their current dilemma on her! "That you're doing me a favor?"

"We're running out of time, Maggie."

She glanced back in the direction they'd come. Part of her wanted to run... Sweet Jesus, why was she hesitating even for a second?

"I don't want you to die because of me."

Maggie tried to drag in a breath, but the new emotion crowded into her chest wouldn't allow the air to reach its destination. Somehow his words struck a chord so deep she could not deny the note of sincerity in his voice. How could he possess such power over her?

Cautiously closing the distance between them, Maggie made her decision. She would do what she had to do in order to ensure her child's survival. Nothing else mattered. Her shoulders reared back and her chin lifted as the air sharply filled her chest. "I'll go along with this for now, but as soon as it's safe I never want to see you again. Is that clear?"

"Fair enough," he agreed.

Slowly, he reached out and took her hand, his strong, warm fingers closing around her cold, trembling ones.

For a fleeting moment they stood as still as stone. Then they ran.

4:20 a.m.

SLADE HAD PUT AS MUCH distance as possible between them and the motel, but Maggie was wearing down. She wouldn't hold out much longer. The police would call in reinforcements in the form of a search team, if they hadn't already. The motel clerk wouldn't be able to provide their names since they hadn't officially registered, but he could provide descriptions. Each passing second could mean the difference between escape and capture. And capture equated to certain death.

Yet, the police were the least of his concerns. *She* wouldn't back off simply because her two hired guns had failed. Her reinforcements would be close behind the authorities. Even if the police took Maggie into protective custody, they would never be able to protect her from the Dragon if she decided she wanted to hurt Maggie just to get to him.

No one could…except Slade, and only if he didn't allow another stupid mistake. He understood this creature who was his mother. Others thought they knew her, but they did not. She was ruthless. Human life meant nothing to her. Nothing was more sacred than the mission.

Maggie stumbled, and Slade caught her before she hit the ground.

"I have to stop a minute." Breathless, she leaned against the nearest tree and wrapped her arms around herself. The wind was cold. Moving had kept them fairly warm so far.

They needed daylight.

Or some better luck.

"Only for a minute." Slade checked his cell to narrow down their position relative to the interstate. The motel hadn't been that far from the highway, but their trek through the woods had, out of necessity, taken them in a different direction. If they could reach the on-ramp before the police issued an APB, they might be able to catch a ride with a passing trucker. Every mile they put between them and Chicago increased their chances of survival.

Slade confirmed the direction they needed to take. "We gotta move." He held out his hand. After a brief hesitation she placed hers there.

Keeping her so close would make what he had to do that much more difficult, but, for now, he had no alternative. Her survival was his responsibility.

The woods were thick, the canopy above scarcely parting here and there to allow a sliver of moonlight. The underbrush made moving forward difficult. Slade cut the path, pushing through the dense growth, allowing Maggie to have an easier go. Chances were she would see this as a thoughtful act when, in fact, it was nothing more than a way to ensure efficiency. If she slowed down or stopped, he would have to, as well.

Half an hour later the woods started to thin. They were close to the highway. Slade moved faster, anticipation stinging through his veins.

"Wait." Maggie tugged against his hold.

"We can't stop." He started forward once more, but Maggie didn't budge.

"Go on without me. The police will find me and I'll swear I don't know which way you went."

Explaining why that wouldn't work would be complicated. They had to keep moving.

Rather than argue, he released her hand and swept her off her feet. With her in his arms, he trudged forward.

"You can't carry me," she argued. She squirmed against his chest.

The feel of her hip grinding into his chest had tension firing in his muscles. "Stop fidgeting and this will go a lot more smoothly." He tuned out the feel of her body. Just as swiftly he banished the images of all those nights they'd spent together in her bed.

Five minutes more and endless gritting of teeth to keep the haunting images at bay and they reached the fence that separated the tree line from the expanse of state-owned right-of-way that ran along the side of the road.

He settled Maggie onto her feet and surveyed the five-foot chain-link wall that stood between them and their destination. Moonlight sifted through the darkness, pooling around their position. The low hum of traffic on the interstate offered the only indication the whole world wasn't asleep.

She wouldn't be asleep. Slade's jaw tightened. She was out there somewhere assessing the feedback and directing every minor reaction as meticulously as a conductor leading an orchestra.

"I'll climb over." Slade pushed aside what he could not control and focused on what he could. He turned to Maggie and pointed to the diamond shapes the metal fencing formed. "Use the pattern as finger- and toe-holds. Once you're up and over, I'll help you down."

She drew in a shaky breath. "All right."

Slade scanned the highway once more, then scaled the fence. He waited on the other side as Maggie slowly climbed the same path. It wasn't that high, but she was a lot shorter than he was, so he understood her trepidation.

When both legs were on his side of the fence, he

placed his hands on either side of her waist. "Let go. I've got you."

There was a hesitation before she followed his instructions. His hands around her waist, he lowered her feet to the ground and she swayed into his chest. He steadied her.

"Thanks." She squared her shoulders and stepped away from him. "What now?"

Slade surveyed the dark highway. "We head toward the on-ramp and flag down a ride." *And watch for the cops,* he didn't add. If they were lucky, an APB hadn't been issued yet and there wouldn't be extra patrols.

"Okay."

To his surprise she began walking before he did.

The motel was only a few miles behind them. The crisscross route they had taken had brought them back around to where they needed to be. He'd kept to the woods until they were near the on-ramp. His instincts nudged him with the urge to run, but he resisted. Maggie couldn't run anymore. They stayed close to the fence, trudging through the knee-deep weeds.

"If you spot any headlights, get down," Slade warned.

"Will the police be looking for us?"

It sounded like hope in her tone. "Yep."

"We can't explain what happened and get their help?"

That would seem like the logical thing to do *if* he were living in a fantasy world. "It's not the police we need to be afraid of."

She hurried a little faster. "If we have nothing to fear from them, why can't they help us?"

"The police can't protect us, Maggie."

She stopped. "I need you to explain that part."

Slade admitted defeat on the issue and turned around.

"Fine. It's not like we're in a hurry or anything." If he hadn't blown a few critical circuits the last couple of years, he would have pulled his weapon and this discussion would have ended already. But, stupidly, he'd allowed complacency to dull his instincts.

"First," he said more loudly and with far more drama than he'd intended, "if I'm not charged with kidnapping and murder, and we're put in so-called protective custody, *she* will have us eliminated. No one can protect us from her. Do you get that? No one." He didn't wait around for her response.

"How can anyone be that powerful? Who is this woman?" Maggie hurried to catch up to him.

Light flickered.

"Down." Slade crouched, tugging Maggie with him.

The headlights grew closer. Not a car. A truck. A big one.

"Go to the side of the road and wave. Maybe the driver will stop. You get the ride and I'll catch up."

Maggie searched his face a moment, then shot to her feet and rushed forward, quickly wading from the knee-deep grass to the recently mowed roadside. She waved her arms, moving closer to the pavement.

There was the possibility that if the driver stopped she could use the opportunity to escape. It was a risk he had to take. Any driver was far more likely to stop for a woman alone.

The truck's air brakes whined as it slowed. As soon as the tractor-trailer came to a complete stop, Maggie rushed to the passenger-side door. She stepped up onto the running board and the window powered down.

Slade braced to run.

Her usually calm voice sounded a little high-pitched.

He couldn't make out what she was saying. She did a lot of gesturing.

"Hurry, Maggie," he muttered to himself.

She reached for the door handle. He moved forward, staying low enough to use the landscape as cover.

As he neared, he heard Maggie saying, "I really appreciate this. I didn't know how much farther I could make it."

Slade dashed across the final expanse of shorter grass and lunged up onto the running board just as Maggie settled into the seat. He had his weapon in his hand before the driver could grab the one stored under his seat.

"We don't want any trouble," Slade advised. "We just need a ride."

The driver glared at him. "What's the gun for, then?"

"Same thing as the one under your seat."

"Can we just go?" Maggie pleaded. "We really do need a ride. That's all."

Slade knew those shimmering green eyes of hers almost as well as he knew his own. He didn't have to see her face as she appealed to the driver; he was well aware just how persuasive those jewel beauties could be. The driver didn't stand a chance.

The man jerked his head toward Slade. "If he puts his gun away, I'll take you as far as St. Louis."

Maggie turned to Slade. He nodded and tucked the weapon into his waistband.

"Let's go," the driver said, turning his attention to the road. "I've got a deadline."

Maggie scooted over, making room for Slade. He slid in next to her and closed the door. The driver let out on the clutch and the big rig roared forward.

Slade monitored the side mirror as they climbed the on-ramp to the interstate. Now all he had to worry about were roadblocks.

"You're the couple the cops are looking for," the man suggested.

Maggie turned to Slade, her eyes wide, her face pale.

"Unfortunately," Slade admitted. Denying the accusation would be a waste of energy.

"Those men tried to kill us," Maggie offered. "They just started shooting." Her words warbled. "We tried to run away, but they came after us."

The driver sent a sideways look at Slade. His sympathies lay solely with Maggie. "I guess you were in too big a hurry to explain things to the police."

Slade put one arm around Maggie's shoulders and rested his other hand at his waist. The truck was gaining speed, which indicated the driver had no plans to try to force them out of the truck. Still, he was making no bones about his suspicions.

"Something like that." Slade exchanged another look with the guy. "Is that going to be a problem?"

The driver shook his head. "As long as there's no trickle-down effect, I got no issue with it."

When the driver had turned his full attention to the road, Slade relaxed.

His contact was compromised, but St. Louis was a big city. He would figure out a new route to his destination.

He wasn't bested yet.

Chapter Five

Maggie roused from a fretful sleep. Where was she? Memories flooded her lethargic brain. Cognizance rocketed into full focus as the details from the passing landscape assimilated in her brain. Streets. Buildings. The beastly sound of the big truck. They'd reached the city. She blinked a couple times and tried to spot something familiar. This had to be St. Louis. Where were they going from here? In reality, she was terrified of what came next. Worry for her baby twisted painfully in her stomach. She ordered herself to try to stay calm. All these crazy emotions couldn't be good for the tiny life just beginning inside her.

She'd finally drifted off before daylight this morning. Her body ached. Her neck was stiff. Tension rippled through her. She'd leaned her head against Slade's shoulder and his arm was around her. As if this recognition had signaled all her senses, she became aware of his scent, the feel of his strong arm, the heat of his body. Every part of her that made her woman wanted to stay right there. To feel safe and protected.

But she was not safe. Maggie straightened, drew

away from him as much as she dared without alerting the driver to the tension. "Are we—" she cleared her throat "—in St. Louis?"

"You got it, Red," the driver announced.

His comment helped to ease the renewed apprehension ramping up. Maggie couldn't begin to count the times she'd been called Red. She'd hated it in school, but, as an adult, she'd finally gotten over it and embraced the overture for what it was—more often friendliness than rudeness.

The driver's name was Pete. Once he'd gotten started talking this morning, he'd poured out his life story. Maggie had fallen asleep at the part where he and his fourth wife had divorced. The man had kids in three states.

As wild as that all sounded, it carried a refreshing normalcy about it.

"I need to fuel up," Pete said as he changed lanes and slowed for the next exit.

Not a hundred yards from the exit ramp, Pete made a right into the parking lot of a massive fuel station. In addition to selling fuel, the truck stop offered a restaurant and showers.

Who knew?

Pete parked the truck in the sprawling lot alongside dozens of other similar rigs. He shut down the engine, heralding a stark quiet that rang in her ears. "I think I might just fuel up myself first. You folks interested in breakfast?"

Slade thrust his hand at the man. "We appreciate the ride, Pete, but we'll keep moving. You understand, I'm sure, our need to cover more ground."

Pete nodded. "Got it. Keep your heads down." He

flashed a smile for Maggie. "Take care of your wife. She must love you a lot to go through all this and stick by your side."

"She's one of a kind," Slade agreed before climbing out of the big cab.

"Thanks, Pete." Maggie returned his smile. She wanted to say more, but the right words escaped her. Instead, she climbed out of the massive truck and turned to the man who had flipped her world upside down.

Slade placed his hand at her elbow and urged her forward. Maggie hated to say anything, but she really needed to use the ladies' room, and her stomach was out of sorts. Several gas stations and no shortage of restaurants, mostly fast food, lined the street. Surely they could make a quick dash into one of them. The smell of food wafting in the air should have been appealing, but the thick odors were anything but this morning.

"Can we get coffee?" She and Slade had been sleeping together for nearly two years. It was foolish of her to be embarrassed about mentioning her personal needs to him, but she was, nonetheless.

"As soon as we're out of eyesight from our friend Pete we'll have breakfast and a break."

Maggie wanted to ask him what came next, but she decided to wait until she had relieved herself and gotten some food into her stomach—if she could manage the latter. She didn't feel well. Prompting additional stress wouldn't be smart right now, she reminded herself. Her hand went instinctively to her belly.

Guilt that she wasn't adequately protecting her child roiled inside her. She wasn't sure how far along she was. This month's skipped cycle would indicate about six or seven weeks. But last month's had been off, almost nonexistent. If she had actually missed two cycles, she would be ten or eleven weeks along. If she survived this scene right out of an action flick, she had only about seven months to go.

The same old questions logjammed in her brain. How had this happened? Did she need to be concerned that she'd taken her pills for some amount of time after conception? She needed to set up a doctor's appointment as soon as possible. There were so many steps that needed to be taken. Assuming she survived this.

She stole a glance at the man beside her. What in the world was she going to do?

He chose a familiar chain restaurant for breakfast. As they entered, the smells of pancakes, eggs and bacon made her stomach rumble, this time in anticipation. Maybe food was all she needed to settle that unpleasant feeling plaguing her. The hostess seated them and promised that a waitress would be with them soon. Maggie excused herself and hurried to the ladies' room.

One look in the mirror and she gasped. Slade had insisted on leaving her purse in her car, so she had nothing to work with. For now, she relieved herself, washed her hands and face, and tried to do something with her hair. Those Irish locks she'd inherited from her great-grandmother were as stubborn as all get-out. She did the best she could, then tidied her clothes.

She was ready. She stared at her reflection in the mirror. Her face was even paler than usual. She licked her lips and took a deep breath.

"What're you doing?" Why didn't she just walk out of here? There were too many people around for him to draw his weapon. He wouldn't want that kind of attention.

Anticipation stirred in her chest. Once she'd explained what happened to the police, she could go home. Take care of the coffee shop. See the doctor. Get on with her life.

The police can't protect us, Maggie. What if he was right? What if this crazy woman tried to use Maggie to lure Slade into some sort of trap? Or killed her?

Maggie's hand went to her belly. She had to protect her child.

Pete, the truck driver, had been wrong. She wasn't going through all this just because she was so madly in love with Slade—which foolishly she was. Maggie's top priority was the baby and until she knew more, she had to assume that Slade was telling her the truth.

Not that he'd ever told her the truth before.

Coffee and water had been delivered to the table by the time she returned. Maggie lowered herself into a chair, placed a napkin in her lap and devoured the water. She hadn't noticed until she took that first sip how immensely parched she was. The cool liquid felt good going down. Chasing it with the warm coffee was equally enjoyable. Relief slowly unfurled, from her rigid shoulders all the way to the aching muscles in her calves. The events of those hours in the dark seemed a little further away.

When she lowered her cup, Slade was watching her. As if a switch had been flipped inside her, she instantly got lost in his eyes. How had she ever allowed herself to get this addicted to a man she had come to realize kept so very many secrets?

"I ordered toast, bacon and eggs, scrambled the way you like," he informed her.

Scrambled eggs. Her mind latched on to those two

words. It was the strangest thing. Here she sat in a public restaurant on the run with a man she clearly didn't know, in a city she'd passed through only on the way to somewhere else, and she got mentally hung up on a point about eggs. She had known Slade Keaton for two years. In all that time, whenever they had shared a meal, he'd eaten whatever she ate. Scrambled eggs, steaks well done, grilled chicken. Whatever. She could not recall him ever ordering anything different from what she ordered. Or ever offering to choose an activity besides what he already knew from experience she liked to do.

"How do *you* like your eggs?"

He looked puzzled by her question.

"You ordered scrambled because that's what I always order or prepare." She fidgeted with the napkin in her lap to busy her hands.

"I like scrambled eggs."

His face blanked the same way it had last night whenever she'd demanded answers. What kind of man couldn't tell the truth about eggs? Hysteria jarred her. She battled it back. "What about steak?" she asked sharply. Again she fought for that calm that seemed to be slipping rapidly from her grasp.

He sipped his coffee, took his time placing the cup back on the table. "The cut?"

Anger entered the emotional mix playing havoc with her control. "Medium? Well done? Rare?"

"Well done."

"How about wine? White or red?" she snapped.

"White." The tiniest lines formed on his brow, suggesting confusion or maybe frustration.

"Whole milk or skim?"

He manufactured a half smile. "You must be starved. All your questions are about food."

Maggie wadded the napkin in her fist. She leaned forward. "You always pick what I pick. Do what I want to do. Even music." Good grief, she'd forgotten that until now. "You like all the music I like." If they went to a museum or gallery, would he gravitate to her same interests? Of course he would. It was all an act. A well-planned and perfectly executed strategy.

The waitress arrived with their breakfast. The smells that had moments ago revved her appetite now had her stomach recoiling. She had to eat. If not for her, for the baby.

Rather than wait for his answer, she took a forkful of food and forced herself to eat. The bacon was crispy, which made it more palatable. Totally ignoring him, she waved down the waitress and ordered orange juice. The server had no sooner placed it in front of Maggie than she drank it down. That really hit the spot. The sweet, tangy liquid awakened her taste buds as nothing else had. When she paused to catch her breath she realized she'd overlooked her toast, but she was stuffed.

Slade stared at her, his food scarcely touched. "I guess you were hungry."

She wanted to argue and say she hadn't been hungry at all, but the baby growing inside her needed nourishment. But she couldn't do that. Fear and worry and excitement had rolled into a ball and started to expand in her chest. An urge hit with such swiftness and such intensity that Maggie barely scrambled from the table and made it to the ladies' room in time to prevent humiliating herself. The lovely eggs and crunchy bacon she had devoured with such fervor exited with equal vehemence.

She sagged against the stall wall. It took a moment or two to steady herself. She unrolled a gob of toilet paper and cleaned up her mess. With monumental effort, she moved to the sink, washed her hands and face, and rinsed her mouth.

After pulling herself together, she made her way back to Slade. He had already placed the cash on the table for their meal.

He stood. "You ready?"

For what? She wanted to ask that but didn't. She knew there was no point. Instead, she nodded and followed him out to the parking lot. The breeze remained chilly, but the sun was shining and Maggie appreciated that very much. She hugged herself and followed him to the gas station next door.

He scanned the parking lot. Mostly passenger automobiles were parked there. The big trucks were piled into the three truck stops that dotted this stretch of street.

"So." She couldn't bear not knowing a moment longer. "What's next on the agenda?"

"A major purchase."

Confused, Maggie asked, "What kind of purchase?"

Slade gestured to the newspaper vending machines near the entrance to the station. "Wait right there."

There were other questions she could have asked. Truth was, she didn't possess the energy to put up a fuss. She took the position and waited.

As long as nothing blew up or no one started shooting, she would go along for a little while longer.

What else was she going to do?

Private Airfield, 12:48 p.m.

SLADE PAID THE GUY THE THREE hundred bucks he'd promised for a ride to the airfield. He watched the van drive away until it disappeared in the distance. Maggie waited silently next to him. She hadn't asked any questions as he'd ushered her into the van back at the gas station. She'd said nothing during the long ride here.

The airfield was in the middle of nowhere well outside St. Louis proper. There was a small box of an office and an adequate strip. A call to the pilot had verified that the private flight reserved for Slade remained on his schedule. The plane sat in front of the only hangar. The pilot was nowhere in sight.

The only question now was whether or not it was a trap. Slade hadn't been able to contact McCain, which confirmed his suspicions that his contact had been eliminated. How much of Slade's transportation plans had been gleaned was anybody's guess. The location of the motel, obviously. But the flight plan? Who knew?

Only one way to find out.

Slade huddled with Maggie. "I don't know what will be waiting in that hangar, so it's best if you wait here until I give the all clear."

"And if it's not clear?"

He placed his secure cell phone in her hand. "Head for the office and call 911."

She held his gaze for a long moment, and he saw the fear in her eyes.

He turned away. No point giving the enemy more time to prep for an ambush.

"Slade."

He shouldn't turn back, but for reasons he would never fully grasp, he did.

"Be careful."

He gave her a nod and resumed his trek toward whatever waited inside.

The hangar doors were open. His hand resting on the butt of the weapon in his waistband, he walked inside. The dead silence and the shadows that lurked around the equipment and tool bins amped up the tension humming inside him. The pilot's name was Hendrix. That he was nowhere to be seen was not a good sign. Slade's instincts rushed to the next level. His fingers tightened on the grip of his weapon.

When a side door opened, Slade froze, his feet wide apart. A man matching Hendrix's description stepped through the doorway, tucking his shirttail into his waistband.

"You Christian?" Hendrix asked.

"That's right." Slade relaxed a fraction. McCain had used an alias for the arrangements. "We ready for take-off?"

"Yes, sir." Hendrix hitched a thumb toward the door he'd exited. "I usually take a relief break before boarding."

Slade nodded. "Understandable." This was a three-hour flight. Maybe more if Slade's plan worked out. He kept an eye on the shadowy area in the far corners of the building. So far he hadn't spotted anything suspicious.

"I'm ready when you are." Hendrix gestured to the aircraft standing by just outside the hangar doors. "I have dinner plans with my fiancée tonight. If I'm not back on time she'll make my life miserable for weeks."

"I'll get my wife and we'll be on our way."

Hendrix frowned. "I thought you were the only passenger."

Slade smiled. They hadn't gotten to this guy. Otherwise he wouldn't have been surprised about a second passenger. Slade shrugged. "My wife decided at the last minute that she wanted to go. You know how it is."

Hendrix laughed. "I do and I'm not even married yet."

With a quick check of the area around the hangar, Slade retraced his steps to where he'd left Maggie. He stopped short and glanced around again.

She was gone.

Hell. He turned all the way around. She appeared around the corner of the office.

He let go the breath he'd been holding.

"The office is closed," she said as she came nearer. "I was hoping there was a restroom."

Slade held out his hand. If she'd called anyone, that could mean trouble. Ten minutes and they would be out of here. Still, ten minutes could be a lifetime when every second counted.

She acted confused at first, then she placed the phone in his hand. The expression on her face warned that she'd sensed his distrust. "I didn't call anyone."

He tucked the phone into his pocket. "There's a restroom inside the hangar."

He waited while she took care of business. The pilot readied the plane. When Maggie joined Slade outside once more, he said, "Let's go ahead and board."

The plane's engine roared to life as they approached. Maggie hesitated and looked to Slade. He waited for her to get right with this step. He'd said all there was to say. This was the only option. He had to assume since an ambush hadn't been waiting that this phase of his arrangements hadn't been compromised. That was the best he could do.

Slade took the steps to the plane first, had a look around inside and then offered a hand to Maggie. When she was inside, he pulled in the steps and secured the door.

"Ready?" the pilot asked.

Slade gave him a nod as he settled in for the flight. Once they approached Mexico City he would give the pilot an alternate airfield for the landing. He wouldn't like it since the change would deviate from the flight plan he'd filed, but he would get over it.

If he didn't, Slade would handle the landing himself. He hadn't operated an aircraft this size, but he was a quick study.

Maggie leaned her head back and closed her eyes. She would have questions. That she saved them for later was fortunate. The pilot didn't need any additional details to pass along if questioned later.

Slade had resources south of the border, but none like McCain. Weapons, ammo, ID, rudimentary gear and ground transportation. Nothing more. Basically, once they hit the ground in Mexico they were on their own. There was one place he felt confident about leaving Maggie, but he had to be sure that avenue was still viable.

Mexico. Under the circumstances, most would be running in the other direction. But not Slade. He fully understood that running would be futile at this point.

Maybe if he were still on his own he could manage. His gaze settled on Maggie. But not now.

Now he had just once chance… Kill the Dragon before she killed him.

Chapter Six

Chicago, 2:00 p.m.

"Lucas."

Lucas jerked from his troubling thoughts. "Yes?" He focused on the faces around the conference table in Victoria's office. "You were saying...?"

Victoria's worried gaze settled on his, and Lucas managed a dim smile. The last thing she needed right now was to worry about him. Simon Ruhl and Ian Michaels, Victoria's seconds in command here at the agency, were briefing them on the Keaton situation. None of the news was good. Lucas felt a cramp of new frustration.

"Jim received confirmation that, thankfully, there were no victims as a result of the explosion," Simon explained. "Only property damage. Unfortunately, that's the only good news we have."

"Still, that's a tremendous relief." Victoria's shoulders sagged, confirming the reprieve she felt at hearing the news.

Ian Michaels picked up the briefing. "Maggie James appears to have vanished. None of her employees has heard from her. Her assistant manager allowed me to check her apartment and it appears untouched. Her personal belongings seem to be in order." He glanced at his notes. "My contact says there have been no transactions on any of her credit cards or her bank card. However, her car and purse were found at the bus station downtown. There was no indication of foul play other than the ominous facts that her keys were in the ignition and her purse was abandoned."

"There have been no public-transportation arrangements in her name or Keaton's," Simon added. "That doesn't mean one of those routes hasn't been utilized. We know that Keaton has operated under numerous aliases."

"What about this woman referred to as the Dragon?" Victoria asked.

That she glanced at Lucas as she stated the moniker twisted the misery already writhing in his gut. He had brought this new menace to Victoria's door. His every effort to determine the threat Keaton represented had proved futile. And it had cost numerous lives. For the first time in his adult life Lucas felt helpless. The admission, even if only to himself, sliced through his heart like a newly forged dagger.

"What about you, Lucas?"

Lucas turned to Ian. Both he and Simon had been with Victoria for a very long time. Either man would gladly lay down his life for this woman. As would Lucas. "I spoke with Thomas Casey this morning." Thomas and Lucas had once worked together in the CIA's most elite covert unit—the Specialists. Thomas was also the uncle of Casey Manning, Lucas's goddaughter. "Based on the incident in Acapulco, the CIA believes she is somewhere in Mexico. For the past ten years there has been no documented activity related to her. Most consider her deceased, as did I. There is no evidence that Keaton is her son or that the woman called Alayna, whom Stark and Casey encountered in Acapulco, is her daughter."

Lucas heaved a weary breath. "That said, there is no evidence to the contrary, either. In fact, outside the club she owned, there is no evidence Alayna exists at all. The same goes for Keaton. What we know of his life here the past two years is all there is, it seems."

Victoria shook her head. "How can this be?"

The worry weighing on his wife hurt Lucas more than any other aspect of this business. That Keaton had obviously taken an innocent victim deeply disturbed him. They had to find Maggie and help her. If she didn't realize the danger around her, she would very soon. Then it might be too late.

"We'll keep you posted on any updates we receive," Simon offered, winding up the briefing.

Lucas thanked both men as they left Victoria's office.

Victoria sat, as Lucas had been minutes ago, lost in her own troubling thoughts. He reached across the table and took her hand. She lifted her gaze to his.

"We will find them. Then we'll have our answers."

"Is *she* the one trying to kill Keaton?"

Lucas wished he could answer that question with any measure of accuracy. "That is the consensus." Victoria knew this the same as he did. There were other questions she wanted to ask. If he was brave enough, he would give her the answers without her having to ask. But just now he lacked the courage to say the words that might in any way hurt her further.

"Is there any chance she will fade into obscurity

like before?" The hope that flickered in Victoria's eyes thrust the knife deeper into Lucas's chest.

"She won't stop until she's finished what she started." That he knew with complete certainty. Though his personal association with her was limited, he knew her reputation well.

Victoria fell silent again. For several moments she seemed lost in thought once more, then she returned her attention to him. "Do you know her name?"

Lucas shook his head. "I can't be certain of anything related to her. In the intelligence-gathering world we work under deep cover, weaving elaborate webs of deception."

"But you had a name for her," Victoria pressed. "She was your lover, Lucas."

The pain in Victoria's eyes ripped at his heart. "Renae. She called herself Renae back then. That name was never officially connected to her. She has many aliases, all dead ends as far as tracking her activities."

"Is it true that she looks enough like me that we could be sisters?"

Lucas had known this question was coming. To her credit, Victoria had not allowed personal feelings to get in the way of what had to be done. Maggie James needed their help. Slade Keaton needed to answer for his deceptions. The Dragon needed to be stopped. At least three countries had extermination leases on her head.

"There was a time when the resemblance was quite striking," Lucas confessed. He thought back to the evil woman with whom he had foolishly allowed himself to become involved, however briefly. "But she's nothing like you, Victoria." He squeezed her hand. "Not in any way. She is pure evil."

"Yet," Victoria acknowledged quietly, "you were still drawn to her on some level."

He swallowed back the bitter taste the memories prompted. "There were times when lines were crossed for the sake of the mission."

Victoria smoothed the pad of her thumb over his hand. "I'm aware that accomplishing the mission required great sacrifice at times."

"That's true." He couldn't allow the question she wanted to ask to trouble her a moment longer. The answer, however, carried baggage of its own. "Victoria." He waited until her gaze was locked solidly on his. "I have loved you from the moment I first saw you." A tiny, weary smile tilted her lips. "But you belonged to my best friend, so for more than two decades, I accepted your dear friendship as gift enough."

Tears welled in her dark eyes. The last thing he'd wanted was to add to her pain.

"I love you, Lucas. I genuinely hope I was worth the wait."

Slowly, not taking his eyes off hers, he drew her hand to his lips and placed a kiss there. "Indeed, I would still be waiting if need be. I would gladly wait an eternity for you."

Lucas would protect her with his life. Whatever sacrifice was necessary…he would keep Victoria safe.

Chapter Seven

Mexico, 5:20 p.m.

Airsickness. Slade thought that was Maggie's problem. Maybe the turbulence was part of the problem. She hoped this morning was no indication of how the first trimester of this pregnancy was going to go. Her sisters had complained at great length about their morning sickness experiences. More bouts like this and Slade might become suspicious. The situation was dire enough; Maggie didn't need him questioning her. She wasn't ready to face that decision.

The truth was, she couldn't say for sure how she would hold up under his questioning. Like an addict, she could resist only so much temptation.

"We'll wait here for a time."

He scanned the street, then crossed to a seedy cantina nestled between a boarded-up shop and a tourist trap. Maggie followed. A cloud of disbelief hovered around her. Here she was—pregnant and fleeing from a danger she couldn't comprehend, with a man she couldn't trust.

A smart woman would have made a run for it back at the motel or the airfield... Apparently she wasn't so smart. Maggie kept hanging on to the thread of remote possibility that there was a perfectly logical explanation for all this. Maybe he was a spy who couldn't blow his cover.

Right, and she was a Bond girl.

Her Spanish ranked right around deplorable. Slade's, on the other hand, was incredible. And not just his ability to speak and to understand the words. He spoke the language as if it were his mother tongue, with flair and confidence. She'd had no idea. Something else to add to her "didn't know" list.

They had hitched a ride from the airfield with a local who traveled among the private airfields on the outskirts of Mexico City picking up what he called gringos and hauling them to the city. For a fee, of course. Considering Maggie would wager her savings that the airfield at which they had arrived—the same one the pilot had resisted diverting to—was *unofficial,* she imagined they were viewed as anything but tourists or business travelers to the guy. Apparently, as long as they paid, that was all that mattered. The most unsettling part was how adept Slade appeared at handling all these by-the-seat-of-his-pants maneuvers.

Slade had instructed the driver to drop them off far from the center of the city. This little neighborhood was definitely way, way off the main street. One last time she surveyed the narrow cobblestone path that was so unlike the streets back home, then she went inside. There were somewhat sleazy areas like this one in Chicago; most big cities had their not-so-charming districts. The broken-down storefronts and graffiti-covered walls, the hustlers on the street, some young enough to be in elementary school, were par for the course in areas like that. The occasional food and trinket shop reminded her of Chinatown back home, only this area wasn't as clean.

Maggie chastised herself for having such a low opinion of a place she'd never before visited. Frankly, all that she'd heard on the news lately about the area contributed to that. Still, she should keep an open mind.

Slade surveyed the vacant tables and gestured to one. "You want something to eat?" He sat down in the chair across from her, the door within his view.

Maggie knew she should eat, but after the unpleasant episode at breakfast and then the trouble in flight, she wasn't so sure she wanted a repeat performance. Besides, who knew what they served in a place like this. Mostly tequila, she imagined. The few patrons stationed around the place appeared to be more interested in the drinks the cantina offered than any food that might be on the menu.

She shook her head. "Maybe later."

"I'll be right back." Slade stood and walked to the counter.

Maggie watched as he ordered two of something. He pulled out his cell phone and took a call. He kept his back to her for most of the conversation, not that she could read lips, but she would have liked to observe his face. Right. Like she could have accurately read anything he allowed her to see there. She was about as good at discerning his thoughts and mood as she was at understanding the local language. She picked up the occasional word here and there but otherwise she was in the dark. The language barrier made being here under the circumstances even more daunting.

Eventually he returned to the table, a bottle of water in each hand. Maggie's throat tightened. Water would be good. She'd had a bottle on the plane, but she hadn't been able to keep it down. Her luck might prove better now that her feet were planted firmly on the ground.

In Mexico.

What would her staff think? They would be frantic. And if one of her sisters happened to call or received a call from one of her employees or the police... Maggie didn't even want to think about that. The last thing she wanted was for her family to worry.

"Thank you." Maggie accepted the offered refreshment. She wanted to ask what happened now, but she'd figured out that he would tell her what he wanted her to know when he wanted her to know it. For now, there wasn't a lot she could do about the situation. That said, her job was to pay attention just in case she found herself on her own at some point before this was over. The idea that Slade could be killed sent a new wave of misery washing over her.

She had been tempted to call for help while she'd had Slade's phone back at the airfield outside St. Louis, but she couldn't bring herself to do it. An ache echoed deep in her chest. She needed to know more about the trouble he was facing. He'd said the police couldn't protect them. When she wasn't in the toilet on the flight, she'd spent a lot of time thinking about how she could help herself and help Slade. She had to call the Colby Agency. If anyone could help them, Victoria and Lucas could. She had watched the Colby Agency in action early last year when the building had been under siege. They had used her coffee shop as a temporary headquarters. No one was better at analyzing and rectifying trouble.

First, she needed to understand what Slade and she

were up against. Then she would have to convince him to go along with the idea. She had a feeling she was dreaming on that part.

"I've arranged for a car and other supplies."

That was a start. "Is *she* here? In Mexico?"

He didn't meet Maggie's eyes. "She's here."

Fear erupted into knots in her belly. "Is that why we're here?"

This time he looked her straight in the eyes. "In part."

She tightened her hold on the bottle to prevent him from seeing her tremble. "What does she want?"

Three, four, then five seconds ticked off. "She wants me."

A crushing sensation settled in Maggie's chest. "You said the less I know the better, but—" she chewed her lower lip "—does she have a score to settle with you? Was there a falling-out between the two of you? Is she angry over something you did?"

He leaned forward, looked down a moment as if searching for patience or perhaps the proper words. "That I'm breathing disturbs her."

Maggie prodded her voice around the lump in her throat. "How long has this been…an issue?"

"Long time." He relaxed into his chair and took a long swallow of the water.

How could he be so relaxed? "You've successfully avoided her all this time?"

He stared at Maggie, analyzing her but giving away nothing of his own thoughts. "You're treading into territory that won't give you the definitiveness you're looking for. It's a waste of energy."

What was that supposed to mean? "Why can't you disappear the way you have before? Avoid the confrontation rather than running straight into it?" If he had avoided her for so many years, he had to have relocated numerous times. Obviously he possessed the necessary skills and resources. Why was he walking right into the fire now?

Those dark gray eyes bored into hers. "There are complications this time. I made a mistake by staying in one place too long. Now I can't run."

She—Maggie—was the mistake he'd made. Misery heaped onto her chest. "What can you do?"

More of those trauma-filled seconds elapsed. Maggie waited on pins and needles. Who was this woman to him? Why did she want to harm him?

"There's only one thing I can do."

Maggie held her breath.

"End this once and for all." He glanced toward the dingy window at the front of the cantina, then he stood. "Our car has arrived."

Like him, Maggie had run out of options, as well.

She trailed behind him, her heart sinking lower with each step.

Coyoacán Borough, Mexico City, 6:40 p.m.

THE SMALL FLAT WAS A BIG STEP up from the motel where they'd crashed outside Chicago. The old woman, Lavena, was not exactly a friend of Slade's but she certainly wasn't an enemy. She had helped him out when he was a kid. He couldn't recall how she had come to be in his life, but she had always been there at least on the fringes. Later, he had returned the favor by providing the resources for renovations to the building that had been in her family for five generations. The city officials had hoped to force her out by condemning the property, then taking it for other purposes. Lavena had shown the bastards but good.

The old woman was well into her sixties by now. Her hair had grown thin and gray and her back stooped, but she could fire a weapon as good as a man half her age.

There was no one else Slade could trust now that McCain was gone. Lavena hated the Dragon. She had her own reasons, which she refused to discuss with Slade. Whatever those reasons, Lavena would like nothing better than to annoy the woman she hated so. She considered keeping Maggie tucked out of reach an honor, and an opportunity to twist the proverbial knife.

As soon as he had Maggie settled, Slade intended to set his own final strategy in motion. He would strike before sunrise. The darkness would give him some advantage. His about-face in strategy would provide an element of surprise. The Dragon would expect him to do exactly as he had always done—run. Find a new place and name and lay low until she found him again.

Not this time. This time he intended to fight to the death.

Striking fast was essential. He would not allow Lavena to be more collateral damage in this war. If her support of Slade was discovered before he completed his mission, she would die. He was not without honor.

He would not let that happen.

The Colby Agency and their allies would have feelers out all over for Maggie and for him. Slade's jaw hardened with fury. They had done more than enough already. He understood their intentions, but they had no idea what they had done.

When this was over, he would send Maggie back to them and he would disappear.

There was nothing for him in Chicago.

The sound of water spraying in the shower seemed to mock his conclusion. He dismissed the notion.

Maggie James had been a pawn, nothing more. He wanted no harm to come to her but that was as far as his attachment went. She would be far better off without him, despite what she might feel at the moment. He was better off alone.

A knock at the entry drew his attention from the closed bathroom door. He moved to the window at the front of the flat near the door. A peek between the drab curtains and Slade confirmed that Lavena's grandson, Ramondo, had arrived with supplies. Slade opened the door and stepped back for the man to enter. He looked to be about twenty. According to Lavena, he took care of maintenance for the flats she rented in the old mission she called home. In addition to the maintenance, Ramondo did errands, all in exchange for a place to live.

Sounded like a hell of a deal to Slade. Nothing he'd ever done for his so-called mother had garnered him so much as a thank-you. More often than not, he'd gotten disciplined for his overabundance of ambition or lack of submission.

Slade thanked the man and secured the door behind him. He took his time putting away the food and other supplies Maggie would need for a few days. Lavena would see to it that she had anything she needed. All Slade had to do was convince Maggie to stay put and not to call anyone until he gave her clearance to do so.

He paused, stared at the jacket she'd left on the sofa. Maggie had worked so hard to accomplish a good life.

She was smart and hardworking and she deserved way better than him. She deserved her life back and the opportunity to find someone who would love her as unconditionally as she loved Slade.

A muscle in his jaw began to throb. No one had ever loved him before. Not the way Maggie did. But he didn't possess the capacity or ability to love her back. Not like that. He felt protective of her and he…enjoyed her body…but that wasn't the same thing.

When she'd had time to think about all this, she would thank him.

MAGGIE TOLD HERSELF TO SHUT off the water. It had long ago gone cold.

But she couldn't move.

Her body ached from deep within. She shook all over as if she were going into shock. Fear writhed like a snake fighting for its life inside her, sending quakes along her limbs. What had she done?

At least one man was dead. *Dead.* She'd told herself over and over that if Slade hadn't killed him he would have killed her. Clearly, the act had been in her defense and yet she couldn't banish the horror. A man was dead because of her association with Slade.

She was in Mexico with no documentation of who she was. No driver's license, no passport, not even a library card. How would she get home? How would she protect her baby? Her insurance card was in her purse back in Chicago. In less than twenty-four hours her calm, predictable life had spiraled out of control. That wasn't entirely true. The spin had started two years ago when Slade Keaton walked into her coffee shop for the first time.

He intended to kill this woman called the Dragon. He claimed he had no other choice. Did Maggie's knowledge of his intent make her an accessory? Dear God, if she found a way to get to the police and warn them, would she be costing Slade his only chance of survival?

What should she do? Tears streamed down her cheeks, hot, salty and devastating. She didn't want the father of her child to die. All she wanted was him out of her life. Denial thrust against her breastbone. If that was true, what was she doing here, aiding and abetting him?

Who was she kidding? She was a victim. He'd kidnapped her. He swore the act had been to protect her, but how could she simply take his word? Every single thing he had told her, including his name, was a lie.

Victim. Maggie closed her eyes. She had promised herself she would never again be a victim on any level, not after the divorce.

She straightened, dared her body to tremble. Reaching for the ancient valve, she shut off the water and grabbed the towel she'd slung over the shower rod. Whatever she had to do to free herself of this nightmare, she would do it. She owed Slade Keaton nothing, least of all her allegiance. This waffling back and forth was stupid and cowardly. She had to be smart and strong.

While toweling off her body, she mentally listed all the reasons she had for walking away from him. The baby's safety. Her own. The life she had built in Chicago. Her family and friends.

What had he offered her? Heartache. Fear. Uncertainty. And all three of those had been doled out to her before this nightmare had even begun. Outrage sparked deep in her soul at the idea of how she had lain awake at night waiting for him. So many, many times. If he hadn't shown she lapsed into a pathetic depression. Her soul hungered for him on every level. She felt as if she were dying without him.

That was what he had done for her.

She draped the damp towel on the side of the tub and reached for the clothes his elderly friend had provided. Cotton slacks and a long-sleeved blouse that, though clean and in good condition, weren't from either of the past two decades. She pulled on the borrowed socks and frowned. Where were her shoes?

Her attention shifted to the door that separated her from him. This flat had only two rooms, a large living area that included a bed in one corner and then this tiny bathroom. He would be out there waiting for his turn to shower.

Anticipation lit in her blood, made her heart pound with hope. She could make a run for it while he was in the shower. Surely he would take five minutes and that would provide a decent head start.

Maggie tugged the hem of the blouse down over the waistband of the baggy slacks. She could do this. In her life before Chicago she had done harder things, if not more dangerous.

All she had to do was stay calm and wait until she heard the spray of water.

A smile tugged at the corners of her mouth as she finger combed her hair. She and her baby would be just fine as soon as they were back at the coffee shop where they belonged. Calling the authorities would be the best strategy. No matter what Slade said, she had to trust the law. The alternative was unthinkable.

She opened the door and a burst of cool air slid over

her. The steam her shower had generated drifted from the bathroom with her. Slade stood at the window, watching through the narrow slit between the curtain panels. He turned to her.

"It's all yours." She dredged up a smile. "I feel tremendously better."

He studied her a moment. A voice in her head screamed at her. *Don't act nervous!* Desperate for something to latch on to, her gaze landed on the fruit lying on the table.

"Apples and bananas!" She moved in that direction, praying he wouldn't notice the high pitch of her voice. "I'm starved."

"There's bottled water and juice in the fridge. There's bread and an assortment of dry goods and snacks. Not exactly what you keep at home, but the closest offerings available."

She held the apple she'd selected so tight in her hand she feared it might be crushed. "You've been shopping." He'd left and she hadn't realized.

He shook his head. "Lavena's grandson, Ramondo, picked up a few things. Enough to keep you comfortable."

He was leaving. All the plans and determination she'd set into place minutes ago drained out of her like freshly brewed coffee pouring unchecked from a machine missing its carafe. He had brought her here to tuck her away until he did what he had to do.

Maggie had no ID, no money except what he'd stuck in her pocket, no phone. She visually searched the room once more to confirm there was no phone. Nope. She had nothing but borrowed clothes and a few days' food supply.

As if sensing her trepidation, Slade moved toward her. She told herself not to watch, not to react, but that was as impossible as telling herself not to breathe.

"Lavena will see that you have anything you need." He stopped right in front of Maggie, so close she could smell the aftershave he'd used yesterday or the day before. The scent was one she knew as well as she knew her own. Maybe better.

"Do not attempt to call anyone until I give you the okay. At that time I'll make arrangements for you to return to Chicago."

Somehow she found her voice. "How can you be sure it's safe for me to stay here?"

"Lavena has helped me out many times. She won't let me down."

Maggie swallowed back the emotion climbing from her chest. "So you're leaving."

"Before midnight."

The nod of her head was a little stilted, but at least she managed a response.

"You will be safe here." He gestured to the apple in her hand. "You should eat. I'll shower and make preparations to move out."

Maggie managed another jerky nod. She watched him cross to the bathroom, her knees threatening to give out any second.

At the door he paused.

Her heart pounded so hard she couldn't hear herself think.

He turned back to her. "This will be over soon. You have my word."

Chapter Eight

Central Mexico, 7:00 p.m.

Camille Marek stood on the balcony of her home and surveyed the vast land that sprawled lazily in front of her. She could just see the tiny peaks of the historic colonial architecture of San Miguel de Allende in the distance. The lush greenery interspersed amid the villages and farmland was some of the most beautiful in all of Mexico. Yet, out here, against the sage-blue mountains, she ruled without the interference of law or government. This rugged terrain had discouraged development, making it perfect for her.

Her fortress was like a castle sitting high above the rest, its position providing a strategic advantage.

The cool air filled her lungs with anticipation. She adored the darkness, relished the emptiness of the terrain that separated her from the populated cities and villages she rarely visited. All she required was here within her dominion.

Nothing could touch her here. Nearly three decades ago she had overseen the building of this fortress. Every detail had been accomplished beneath her watchful eye to provide absolute security and privacy. The position at the base of the mountains had provided numerous possibilities for unexpected egress, including air transport to her state-of-the-art yacht.

The cutting-edge surveillance system's perimeter around the property was one hundred meters. Between the cameras, the motion sensors as well as the armed guards, there was little or no possibility of an unexpected breach.

Fury obliterated her sense of contentment. But *he* knew the security measures forward and backward. Though he had turned his back on her and his home a dozen years ago, he had made it a point to stay apprised of any changes. She had discovered this fact only recently. He monitored her moves in order to stay one step ahead. All these years she had known he was out there, despite his having faked his death in hopes of escaping her wrath.

Had she known thirty years ago what she knew now, she would have drowned him as an infant. What an infinite waste of her time and resources he had been. Her lips tightened in escalating rage. She had done everything for them, he and his sister. Only Alayna had properly shown her respect and gratitude. She lived to serve, as it should be.

Camille drew in a deep, resolute breath. Terminating his pathetic existence would move her as much as squashing a trespassing insect. He had been dead to her for many years. His own selfish motives had lured him to turn his back on her, despite all that she had given him. The sentence for such betrayal could be nothing less than death.

She would not allow him to destroy all that she had accomplished. The Code was an unmatched project.

Others had tried and failed. They had not been willing to sacrifice as she had. Her entire life had been dedicated to this one cause. He would not take that from her.

Anyone who got in the way would suffer the same fatal destiny.

She thought of Lucas and a new fury ignited inside her. His tampering was a mistake. One he would regret very soon. A smile tipped her lips. She had so enjoyed the fascinating report of the events during Lucas's recent visit to Mexico. Her loyal servant had relayed how Lucas and his wife had fought to save not only their lives, but those of others. It seemed Lucas had not changed. Too bad for him and his cherished wife. Unfortunately, loyal servant or not, the lone survivor of those she had sent to teach Lucas a lesson about interference had been exterminated. His allegiance had served him well until the very end. A quick message to the authorities where he was being held had resolved that loose end without the slightest delay.

Of all her sexual conquests, Lucas was the only one who had intrigued her so. Perhaps because she had sensed a like spirit in terms of relentless determination and the need to accomplish the mission no matter the cost. That had been their singular common conviction. Lucas Camp was plagued with the one weakness she had never possessed: the need for justice. Did he not realize that all were not created equal? There were three types of humans: prey, survivors and predators. If one was not a predator, then one was either merely a survivor or the food that fueled the top of the food chain.

Predator suited her perfectly.

Camille walked back inside, the heels of her stilettos clicking on the stone floors. She entered her chamber with the intent of checking the status of the numerous ongoing endeavors under her watch. An array of monitors lined one wall, each a running report on the missions under her dominion. Camille required constant updates. Therefore, similar monitors had been installed in every space she frequented. She hesitated at the towering mirror that stood against the wall at the entry to her private rooms.

Maintaining her figure as she neared the mid-fifty mark had not been an issue. Immense self-discipline was one of her most prized assets. She trained as hard as any member of her team. No one was better. Strength was absolutely essential to remaining at the top of the food chain. Weakness, physical or mental, could not be tolerated.

She studied her face. Decades ago she had gotten used to this face. It represented one of her many masterpieces. Her greatest triumph despite the failure in the end. No matter, there would be other successes. She would need to stay at her very best. Meticulous care was necessary to stay youthful looking. She had changed her hair some years back. It no longer draped around her shoulders. The more sophisticated, shorter style was far more to her liking. Pleasing to the eye.

She touched her cheek, soft and supple. No matter the extent required to retain her youth. What would *he* think when they came face-to-face? And they would. She knew Lucas. He would not rest until he had confronted the threat to his perfect world. How would he react when she told him the truth he would not want to hear? She had watched him and his wife in Puerto

Vallarta. He had seen Camille, but only for a second. Just long enough to make him sweat. A smile toyed with her lips. Oh, how she wanted him to writhe with worry. He and that precious wife of his, the esteemed Victoria Colby.

The smile teasing her lips stretched wide. She relished the thought of causing him pain. She held out her right hand and admired the beautiful ring she always wore. Ornate titanium setting with a massive rubylike stone. In the same way as her home, she'd had the ring designed especially for her. She never took it off.

Her gaze lifted to her reflection once more. Oh, yes, she looked forward with great anticipation to coming face-to-face with Lucas again. For all these years she had been satisfied with their brief encounter so very long ago. After all, she had accomplished the most important feat of her career. There had been no reason to end his existence. The need to utilize him again one day had always been a viable possibility. But he had interfered, trespassed into her world. For that transgression, he would pay. No one crossed the Dragon.

Alayna's image appeared in the mirror. Camille's gaze connected with her daughter's. Generally, seeing her daughter, especially here, was a pleasure—one of the few she allowed herself. But if Alayna were here to plead her brother's case yet again, Camille was not sure she could withhold punishment. She had her limitations, even with her most prized possession.

"You are so beautiful, Mother." Alayna smiled. "Far more beautiful than me."

Irritation sizzled inside Camille. Though sincere, the words were ultimately a precursor to the plea Camille would not again entertain. She turned to her daughter.

"Do not test me, Alayna. I will not tolerate your continued obsession with your brother. He is dead to us. Terminating his existence will protect us. That is all that matters. Do you understand?"

Alayna nodded. "I understand."

That she did not persist raised a red flag. Camille knew her daughter. "It is not wise to hide things from me, Alayna. You are my one and only. I do not wish to lose you as I did the others."

Fear flared in Alayna's eyes. This pleased Camille immensely.

"He has put us at risk." Camille righted a single hair that had fallen out of place. "He has put everything at risk. He must be terminated. There is nothing more I can do except vanquish the risk."

Her daughter nodded again. "You're right, Mother, I know." She looked away. "But you had such high hopes for him. It seems a shame to waste such assets."

He was special, that was true. A relentless intelligence gatherer. A ruthless assassin. Fully capable of eluding the most dogged search. Those skills that Camille had once felt such pride at watching in action were now a threat to her work and to her survival.

Her son had to die.

Chapter Nine

Slade checked his backpack one last time. Ramondo had done well. Slade had everything he needed. Two hand-guns, sufficient ammo, a couple of surprises the Dragon would not be expecting and the necessary papers under a new alias. Not to mention he had ground transporta-tion.

She would be watching, expecting him.

His *mother*. Slade hadn't called her *mother* since he was twelve years old. That was the day she'd terminated the older of the other two. Slade's brother, even if not by blood. She'd chosen Slade's birthday so that he would not forget the price of failure.

"You have everything you need?"

Maggie hadn't said much since his three-minute shower. He'd hurried through the task, leaving the door open to make sure she understood he would know if she tried to make a run for it. Ramondo would be watch-ing, as well. This part was difficult for her, but she would be safest this way. Allowing her any closer to the danger could prove a costly mistake. Though he could not eradicate all risk, his confidence that she would be safe here was somewhat more solid. One day she would understand. Her friends at the Colby Agency would explain to her that he'd made the right decision.

He banished thoughts of the Colby Agency. There was nothing there for him. He'd made a mistake seeking them out. The past two years had been a calculated error. He dismissed the denial that nudged at him.

"Yes." He faced the woman who stood in the middle of the room looking frightened and worried. The idea that her worry was as much for him as for herself aroused unfamiliar feelings in him. No one, except maybe Alayna, had ever cared whether he lived or died. The Dragon's only concern had been whether or not he completed the mission. Whether he survived was irrelevant.

"Are you leaving now?"

The fear in her eyes prompted doubts he shouldn't feel. He picked up his cell from the table where he had it charging, and checked the time, mostly to avoid looking at her. "I have a couple hours yet."

"Why does she hate you so?"

Not responding, Slade crossed to the kitchenette and poured a cup of coffee. Again, more to prevent having to meet her gaze than for the caffeine. He was weak right now. Weary with changing lives too frequently and weak from the mistake of allowing himself to believe he could have what others had. What a joke. He had watched Maggie until his curiosity turned to admiration and then to yearning.

He was a fool to believe that kind of life could be his. The potential did not exist in him.

"You're leaving," Maggie went on. "What difference

does it make if you tell me? I need to know since...I probably won't see you again."

The words echoed in his brain like the rat-a-tat-tat of a machine gun. They shook him to the core.

She wouldn't see him again. That was what she wanted and it was the best decision for both of them. She deserved her life back. If he hadn't been such a fool, this situation wouldn't have happened.

Slade turned to her, leaned against the counter and elbowed aside the foreign emotions just looking at her generated. What was the harm in giving her a glimpse of the truth? Maybe he owed her that much.

"When I was six she taught me to disassemble and reassemble six different weapons, one for each year of my life." He forced down a slug of coffee, the memories making the effort more than a little difficult. "Whenever I made a mistake, she held my head under the water. She would do a series of six dunks, five seconds more each time I screwed up." Instinctively, he sought that place where he felt nothing—a place more familiar to him than his birth name. The first few times she'd dunked him, he had come up from the water screaming. Eventually he'd learned to utilize that fleeting moment to drag air into his lungs. His fingers clenched around the cheap stoneware cup. "It didn't take me long to get it right every time."

Horror gathered like storm clouds in her expression. Her arms visibly tightened around her waist. "You were just a child!"

He laughed, the sound dry and riddled with disgust, as much with himself as his so-called mother. "By the time I was ten I was an expert marksman on any weapon I was big enough to hold. I learned hand-to-hand combat, the proper use and disposal of explosives. She had moved on, as well. To different techniques to punish my mistakes." A smile edged its way into the corners of his lips. "You see, I learned to hold my breath so well and for so long that her water torture no longer worked. That she couldn't use that to terrify me infuriated her."

Maggie's breath caught as realization dawned. "The scars."

He downed more of the coffee. They had talked about the scars. He had told her he'd been in an accident, but that had been just another of his stock responses. "Torture techniques are one of her specialties. The slower the better."

Maggie walked slowly toward him. He tensed. Having her touch him…having her make him feel anything else would be treading into dangerous territory. She reached out and placed the palm of her hand over his heart. "What about this?"

Heat from her palm warmed that icy place. "That's where I had a tattoo removed." The memory of that long-ago day, when she had branded him, caused his fingers to curl with the need to choke her. He would not fail with this last mission.

A frown furrowed her brow. "Why that one? You have other tattoos."

He did. *Liberty or Death* on his left biceps. *Solitary* on his back. But those were different. He had chosen those. The other had been her mark. "She branded some of us." That was a monumental understatement but close enough.

"Us?"

"Her chosen ones." His chest convulsed even now,

after all these years. "The ones who made up the Code."
He clamped his mouth shut. That part he should have
kept to himself. That single word could cost Maggie her
life. But it was too late. He couldn't take it back. She
would never let it go so easily.

"What does that mean?" Her hand dropped to her
side. "What kind of code?"

He finished off the coffee and moved around her.
"I've already said too much." What the hell had he been
thinking? That he wanted her not to hate him…not to
think he was a monster for no real reason. The truth
was, he was more monster than man. Maggie James
had merely seen what he'd wanted her to see.

She should hate him. Like all the pawns he used, she
had no idea the things he had done in his life. If she
knew just a fraction, she would recoil in disgust.

"There was no one to stop her? Did anyone even
try?" The misery in her voice tugged at him, made him
want to be wrapped inside the compassion she offered
for the child he had never been. No one had been there
to save him. He had been completely alone with pure
evil. No one had cared. Least of all his *father*. Fury
twisted in his gut. He shook his head. Speaking would
only reveal more of that uncharacteristic weakness.

"Why did she do this?"

This had gone far enough. She had traced his steps
and waited right behind him, the sweet, innocent smell
of her, the feel of her body so close, tugging at his
senses. Why did he torture himself?

"Why would she teach a child those things? It's…
it's insane."

Her shock or maybe her too-logical question
prompted another of his fake laughs. "She created the

perfect team of infiltrators and assassins." He turned to see her face. He wanted to see the disgust. Maybe that would stop these alien sensations hurtling through him. "I can't even remember the number of people I've killed, much less their names or faces." She had taught him not to look. He could see without looking, she would say.

The disgust he'd expected failed to make an appearance on Maggie's face. Instead, he saw sympathy, pain, compassion. He had to look away.

"Why didn't anyone stop her?"

Enough. He rounded on her, anger blasting through him. "Because she killed anyone who got in her way." Another of those laughlike sounds burst from his throat. "The one person who could have stopped her was missing in action."

Maggie flinched, but she held her ground. "Who is this woman? Who gave her that much power over a child?"

Slade hesitated.

"Tell me," she demanded. "Who is she? How did you end up with such an evil woman?"

Maggie was mad as hell on his behalf. He was thirty years old and not once in his life had anyone looked ready to tear apart a lion in his defense.

"She's my mother."

The shock and horror chased away the anger and outrage. Maggie blinked, opened her mouth to speak, but apparently couldn't find the words she wanted to say. Then she licked her lips and Slade didn't care if she said anything at all.

He needed to taste her. To obliterate the memories and the hatred with her sweetness...her softness.

Closing the one step between them, he swept her into

his arms and crushed her mouth with his. The fresh taste of fruit and milk made him want to eat her alive. Her body's soft mounds and lean valleys melded with the hard plains of his own. Arousal was instantaneous. He wanted to drink in all of her. To lose himself completely inside her.

She resisted at first, then she turned pliable. His hands roved over her backside, catching the hem of her blouse and dragging it up and over her head. He dropped the blouse to the floor and filled his palms with her unrestrained breasts. The feel of her erect nipples urged him on. She wanted him. She always wanted him.

Slade carried her to the bed. The mattress was old and lumpy, but the sheets were clean. She whimpered as he peeled off her socks, first one, then the other. The pink polish on her toenails made him ache with need. Maggie kept her fingernails short and neat for working in the coffee shop, but her toenails always blazed with sexy color. He lifted her foot and nibbled at her toes. She gasped, her eyes wide with desire.

Slowly, he wiggled and dragged her slacks down her body, then tossed them aside. Her legs were long and silky, her creamy skin already flushed with the same fire blazing along his every nerve ending.

He licked her delicate ankle, measuring the fragility of her small size. Her fingers fisted in the sheet as he kissed his way up her calf, then her thigh. Her legs were toned yet velvety, and he liked the way she wrapped them around him. There was no part of her he didn't savor when they made love. He explored the juncture between her thighs with his tongue and lips, craving more even as her flavor filled him.

Her bottom reared off the mattress, soft moans issuing from her throat. He trailed his tongue over the slight rise of her mound and lapped at her quivering belly. Tracing each elegant rib, he made his way to her breasts. His body stretched along the length of hers, he paused to admire her lush breasts. Perfect, pale mounds topped with firm, crimson peaks. He squeezed each one in turn, watching her pink lips part in desperate longing. One nipple at a time, he suckled until she cried out. Her body writhed with the escalating waves of fulfillment. He reached down and nuzzled a finger inside to feel the contractions of completion throbbing inside that wet heat.

His body shook with the need to be deep in that intense, pulsing heat.

MAGGIE'S EYES DRIFTED OPEN. She fought for breath. Her body hummed with satisfaction even as new waves of need began to build inside her. He was touching her, moving his fingers between her legs in a way that fore-shadowed what she knew would come next.

She wanted to tell him to hurry. To give her what she needed. But she couldn't find her voice. Her hands roamed over his still-clothed body. She wanted his clothes off, his naked skin against her. She needed that thick length inside her.

Pushing against his chest, she rolled him onto his back and straddled him. Those intense gray eyes steamed with his own desire. He might pretend not to need her the way she needed him, but Maggie knew better. She freed one button after the other until his shirt was loose. Pressing her most intimate place solidly onto his, she leaned down and kissed his chest, nuzzling each scar, especially the large one over his heart where he'd removed the tattoo that had branded him as belonging to that evil woman.

Damn her for what she had done to him. His mother! He didn't belong to her. He belonged to Maggie. If she never saw him again, they would have this night. And in her heart, he would always belong to her. The past didn't matter one bit to her. This moment was all they would have, and she wanted it to count.

Her fingers felt clumsy as she unfastened his jeans. The urgency for another release swelling in her had shifted to the need to give him that mind-blowing bliss. To make up for the pain he had suffered in the past. She wanted him to know what unconditional love felt like.

And she did love him. She would never stop loving him. No matter the ugly secrets she learned. No matter what happened tomorrow.

She scooted down the length of him and removed his shoes and socks. Then she tugged his jeans down, revealing a lean waist and narrow hips, and then lower along well-muscled legs. When the jeans joined his shirt on the floor, she gave him the same attention he'd given her. She kissed her way up his powerful legs. She closed her eyes and relished the memories of those strong legs planted between hers night after night.

He was fully aroused, hard and hot. Ready to fill her like no man before him. She took him into her mouth as deeply as she dared. His body tensed, muscles bunching in anticipation beneath her touch. She worked her way up and down, drawing on him with every push and pull of her lips.

He grabbed her by the shoulders and pulled her mouth up to his. The flavor of him mingled with the essence of her as their kiss turned desperate. She sucked his tongue deeper into her mouth. He rolled her onto her back and parted her legs with one knee. Her legs went around his sinewy waist and he planted himself fully and deeply inside her.

She closed her eyes and lost her breath. For long seconds he held still, allowing her muscles to stretch enough to accommodate him completely. Then he moved. Slowly at first, then hard and fast, with that ferocity that nearly terrified her. But her mind reeled too wildly with spiraling ecstasy to truly be afraid. She wanted him. All of him. As hard and fast as he wanted to give himself to her. Later the fear would trickle in to mix with the worry and regret. But not now.

Her fingers dug into his back, her teeth clamped down on her lower lip to hold back a scream of animal pleasure. The waves of desire built, higher and higher, until they crashed over her and she fell into that place of sheer ecstasy, unable to do anything but drift along with every beat of their hearts, every rush of friction between their bodies.

He stopped, stone still. Her entire body went rigid in protest.

She squeezed him. "Don't stop," she urged. She wanted more. He was leaving and she needed this to be enough…to last for the rest of her life. Tears abruptly burned her eyes. He was leaving. She would never see him again. What if he didn't survive this coming battle?

The child she carried would never know him.

He kissed her eyes, her nose, her trembling lips. Then lower. Her breasts were so tender that his every touch, every suckle had her crying out. He brought her to the brink of climax yet again with nothing more than his lips and his tongue. His fingers traced every curve, every rise, soothing each place his mouth tortured so exquisitely.

When she could take no more, he plunged into her over and over until she came apart in his arms. Every cell detonated with fiery pleasure before melting beneath him. He groaned with his own climax, stroking in and out until they had both experienced the last inkling of physical gratification.

Long minutes passed before her respiration returned to normal and her mind worked again. She lay in his arms, her skin soaking up the warmth of his. Her fingers trailed small patterns on his chest. Touching him completed her in a way that wouldn't be easy to live without. How could she let him go? But how in the world could she hope to stop him?

"I still don't understand. Why didn't someone stop her?" she whispered. Child Protective Services, the police, anyone.

His body stiffened in that way it always did when he emotionally withdrew, but he didn't pull away from her physically as she had expected him to. Still, the long moment of silence that followed warned that he might not respond at all.

"There was no one to stop her. No school officials because I was schooled by her. No police because she lives above the law."

Dear God, what kind of monster would do this to her own child? "But you got away?"

"When I was eighteen."

"You've been running from her all that time?" She laid her head against his chest. What a nightmare for him.

"Not running from her, not really."

Maggie held her breath, prayed he would confide in her. Two years she had waited for this.

"I was running from who I was." He stroked her shoulder, slid his palm along her rib cage and over her hip. "From what she made me."

Maggie squeezed her eyes shut to hold back the tears stinging in her eyes. She summoned her courage. "There's no other way to stop her?" If he confronted her, she would have him killed without ever lifting a hand. Maggie hated her and she'd never even seen a picture of her, much less met her.

He shook his head. "This is the only way."

Fear strangled Maggie's heart. Her lips parted with the need to tell him her secret, but she stopped. She couldn't do that. If he came back to her it had to be because he wanted to be with her.

"Nothing I can say or do will change your mind?" Again she held her breath. They could go to the Colby Agency and ask for help. And what about the men who worked for him at his Equalizers shop? Couldn't they help? Maggie banished the memories of the brownstone exploding. The explosion—all of this—felt surreal.

Slade untangled himself from her and got up. Her body grieved the loss. "Believe me, Maggie, in time you'll be glad I'm gone."

Maggie watched as he gathered his clothes. She bit back the words that pricked the tip of her tongue. *Not in this lifetime.*

As much as she wanted to put him and all the lies behind her, being glad about losing him was never going to happen.

Never.

Chapter Ten

Slade watched Maggie sleep. She'd struggled to stay awake, but exhaustion had won the battle. In the end she'd curled into the covers, pulling the blanket up to her chin. Seated next to her on the edge of the bed, he clenched his fingers to resist touching that tousled red mane. Her hair was thick and curly and smelled of the fruity shampoo she used. The silky feel of it made him ache to thread his fingers through it over and over again.

Maggie was the first woman he'd allowed so close. Two years he had worked to seduce her, drawing her ever closer. At first, the step was nothing more than a positioning strategy. Her coffee shop was located directly across the street from the Colby Agency. As time passed and she became more vital to his strategy, he'd found himself noticing things about her he'd never bothered to notice about the other women he'd encountered, whether by chance or by design.

The tiny crinkles around her eyes when she laughed. Her pale, soft skin that was such a contrast to her fiery red hair and dazzling green eyes. It made her look so delicate, so fragile when, in fact, she could be a lioness if the need arose. Her employees adored her, yet Maggie could with a single word or look put an errant one on his or her toes. All who knew her respected her resilience and determination. Yet there was a compassion for others glowing inside her that easily matched the passion with which she lived. And she loved him so completely. How was that possible?

His chest tightened. Her smile, wide and uninhibited, enthralled even him. He liked her smile, missed it when they were apart. That confession rattled him. How had this happened? He had been taught from birth not to feel any sort of weak emotion. He'd never loved anyone. Maybe his sister, though he wasn't sure. He certainly felt protective of Alayna. Long ago he had stopped missing her in his life. It wasn't safe to have any kind of contact with her, though she always knew how to reach him. Before he left they had made a pact to come to each other's aid whenever and wherever necessary. But was that love? Maybe on some level.

Slade stiffened his spine. What he felt for Maggie was similar. He had grown accustomed to her presence in his life. Certain things about her had become undeniably familiar and comfortable. He'd been too human, too weak to resist them, and that had been a mistake. He had put her in danger by allowing this attachment.

It was best to sever that connection. Now. She would recover and forget about him in time.

The sharp stab of pain that pierced his chest forced the air from his lungs. He stood and forced his attention away from her. If he left while she slept she couldn't attempt to dissuade him. Besides, he had several hours of hard driving between him and his destination. Arriving in darkness would serve his ultimate purpose.

As if he hadn't already done so, he checked the three windows in the flat to ensure they were secure. There was only one door; he would lock that on his way out. Slade counted out a sufficient amount of cash, some U.S. dollars, some pesos, and tucked the folded bills into Maggie's shoe. Everything she needed in the way of food supplies was here. The idea of leaving her unarmed was less than appealing, but if she couldn't use it, a weapon in her hand was more dangerous than being unarmed. In the time that he had known her she appeared to abhor guns. Anyway, both Lavena and Ramondo were armed.

With one last look at her he walked out the door and locked it behind him. With the backpack on one shoulder, an automatic in his waistband, he drew in a deep lungful of night air and pushed all other thought from his mind except his mission.

Penetrate the fortress and end this once and for all.

Slade scanned the street as he descended the steps leading down from the second-floor landing outside the flat Lavena had provided. The old woman's first-floor flat was dark, as was Ramondo's. Lavena and her grandson lived in two of the three first-floor units. The other they used for storage and God only knew what else. Year-round tenants rented the remaining two on the second level. Lavena kept one open for an occasion such as this, though she would never admit as much. She liked coming off as hard and unfeeling. Slade knew the woman too well to be fooled. There was a softness inside her. He didn't fully understand its origin or why she directed any aspect of it toward him, but it was there just the same.

Deep down, Lavena had always hoped Slade would

return to Mexico and call her neighborhood home. Maybe he had been wrong when he'd considered that Maggie was the only woman who'd ever got so close. Lavena had done the same, only Slade had been a kid and the relationship had been a strange twist of protectiveness and revenge. Lavena would do anything to infuriate the Dragon. That was the only reason he trusted her with Maggie's safety and with providing the resources for his mission. Keeping Maggie a secret and safe from the Dragon would prove a major coup for Lavena. She would revel in bragging how she had protected Maggie once this was over.

It was nothing short of a miracle that she had escaped the Dragon's wrath all these years.

Slade stood in the darkness, the past swirling around him like fog. Nothing about his past was normal. Nothing. Certainly not his childhood. Actually, using that term in context with his history on this earth was a total joke. He hadn't had a childhood. He'd had training. He hadn't gone to school. What he'd learned was topographical maps and strategic maneuvers and infiltration techniques.

He stared up at the dark sky and wondered, for the first time in as long as he could remember, why him? Who had decided that his life would be filled with pain and punishment?

Slade shook it off and focused on the mission. Nothing else mattered. He was trained to ignore all else. Now was no different. This temporary faltering would pass soon enough.

As if some rebellious brain cell had suddenly decided to show its stubborn side, his gaze shifted back to the door of the flat where Maggie slept.

Her life had been normal until he invaded her contented little world. She'd grown up with loving, nurturing parents and a couple of siblings who had maintained a close relationship with her. A few rough knocks had shaken her, like a jerk of an ex-husband, but she had bounced back. Fury burned in Slade's gut. What kind of man would take for granted a woman like Maggie?

Maybe a guy a lot like Slade. Who was he to condemn anyone else?

No one.

His list of previous existences included dozens of names and twice as many places. None of which had been real.

Slade closed out the nagging memories.

A light appeared in Lavena's front window. Had she been watching for him to leave? Palming the weapon, he moved toward her door. Two steps from the threshold, the door opened. Lavena, clad in a ratty housecoat, looked him up and down.

He waited. She said nothing. "What?" he demanded.

She eyed him a moment longer. "She's going to kill you, you know."

He'd heard that before. "She'll try."

Lavena shook her head. "It's different this time."

Slade felt his eyebrows hike upward. "You're getting old, Lavena. And sentimental."

She laughed, a gravelly sound. "Maybe. Hit sixty-seven this year. Guess that makes me old enough to know what I'm talking about."

"Perhaps," he agreed.

Even now Slade marveled at her perfect English and the total lack of a discernible accent. Like him. Though she had lived here her whole life, she could move anywhere on the planet and no one would be able to connect her with Mexico, not by her spoken words or her looks. She could be anyone's grandmother, most anywhere. His training ensured him the ability to fit in anywhere, to gain the trust of those around him in most any situation.

Though he hadn't fooled Lucas Camp. The man was like Lavena. There was something soft, almost out of place, on the inside, but a hard core on the outside. Lucas Camp had sensed some underlying threat to his world as soon as he and Slade met.

Lavena was cunning, too. He couldn't deny her assessment of his current position. This time was different. The goal of his mission was as much about Maggie's survival as his own. Maybe more. The realization was startling on some level. Over the past twenty-four hours he had owned that weakness. No use denying it.

To some extent it was different this time because he was different. The extreme black-and-white-only view he had carried for his whole life was now muddied with expanses of gray. "Take care of her. See that she leaves the country in the same condition she arrived."

Slade started to turn away, but Lavena's next words stopped him. "You could take her and disappear. You know how better than anyone I know."

He closed his eyes and brutally dismissed the reckless voice that screamed at him to listen to the old woman. "She has a life in Chicago." His gaze settled on perceptive brown eyes. "She would never be happy in my world. It wouldn't be enough."

"Have you asked her?" Lavena tightened her sash, as if that move would protect her from the cold night air that had her thin shoulders shaking. "She seems to care a great deal about you. You might want to ask before you make her mind up for her."

Slade hitched the backpack a little higher on his shoulder. "She'll forget about me in time." He refused to allow that truth to pain him again. It was time to go. This exchange was unproductive.

Lavena shook her head. Her dark hair had long ago gone gray. It hung over her shoulder in a long, loose braid. "You've always been stubborn. She ruined you just like she did the others."

How did she know about the others? He'd never heard her talk of them before. But opening that door would only delay what he had to do. "Goodbye, Lavena."

She waved him off. "Go, then, but watch your back."

"I always do."

"Just remember," Lavena called after him, "she's waiting for you. This time one of you will die. If it's you, your woman might never be safe. She could decide to hunt her down, Marek, just to be sure that all signs of you are completely erased."

Slade kept walking, the name she'd called him ringing in his ears.

Marek.

He swallowed back the bile that rose in his throat.

She had given him that name, Tripp Marek. He was not that man anymore.

He was no one. Nothing.

Except the man who was going to kill the Dragon.

2:45 a.m.

MAGGIE'S EYES FLUTTERED OPEN. The room was dark. And too quiet.

Where was she?

Mexico.

She sat up, the air expelling from her body in a rush. "Slade?"

Silence answered her.

He was gone.

Emotion welled inside her, stinging her eyes and making her chest hurt.

When she'd gathered her composure, she pushed the covers aside and dropped her feet to the floor. She threaded her fingers through her hair, thrusting it out of her face. She regarded the dark room with a long, slow look.

"Okay, Maggie, what now?"

She had been ready to banish him from her life. The middle-of-the-night trip to the brownstone had been about closure. The end. Instead of following through, she'd followed him here. She looked around the dark room. He'd killed a man to save her life. They'd fled from the police at a murder scene, and that didn't even count being persons of interest in the explosion. Dear God, what was she going to do? No matter how many times she asked herself that question, the answer never magically came to her.

She got to her feet and straightened her clothes. Sitting here wouldn't help. She had to do something. Where were her shoes? Maggie felt around the floor with one foot. There. She burrowed her left foot into the shoe, then the right. She frowned and kicked off the right. She clicked on the bedside light and checked the shoe. What the heck? She stared at the wad of cash in her hand. He'd left her more money.

Shelter, food, more cash. He had provided everything she needed but a phone. Maggie dropped back onto the bed. He wanted her to hide out here until it was safe. Just sit here and wait to hear if he was dead or alive. She closed her eyes against the thought of him being killed. But the risk was too great to expect anything else.

Maggie was no cop, but even she recognized that the woman he was going up against was powerful and evil. The explosion and the ambush were proof enough. There was no way Slade stood a chance against resources like that. She would kill him.

Her own son.

Pushing back to her feet, Maggie made her decision. She had to do something more than debate herself about this. Before it was too late.

Victoria and Lucas would know what to do. Maggie had become friends with the folks at the Colby Agency. They were the best.

Slade considered Lavena a friend of sorts. Surely with him gone Maggie could help her see reason. It was three o'clock in the morning and the older lady likely wouldn't be thrilled about being disturbed, but Maggie couldn't wait.

She pulled on her jacket and stuffed the money into her pocket. The baby she carried was counting on her for protection. Still, Maggie feared that she might be the only hope Slade had.

Whether he realized it or not.

She peeked out the window and surveyed the street. Dark and deserted. A few cars were parked along the block. There wasn't a single light on in any of the neighboring buildings.

She wished she had a weapon. A baseball bat like the one she kept under her bed back in Chicago. Or a can of pepper spray like she carried in her purse. A quick search of the apartment confirmed that there was nothing she could use as a weapon. She'd just have to work with what she had—her wits.

Several seconds passed before she had the nerve to unlock the door. The thunder of her pounding heart deafened her. She drew open the door far enough to confirm that there was no one on the second-floor landing. Quiet. Deserted. Whoever lived in the other two apartments on this floor didn't seem to be home. There hadn't been a sound or lights earlier and there wasn't any now.

Moving down the stairs was the hardest part. She felt like an open target. Watching the street for trouble, she had to hang on to the railing to keep from stumbling. Once she reached the ground level, she paused to listen. Quiet. Cold. No shadows flitting around.

Lavena's flat was the one directly beneath the one assigned to Maggie. She eased toward the door, afraid to stop looking around even for a second. The windows of the flat were dark. She almost hesitated, hating to wake the woman, but there was no time to wait. Maggie steadied herself and raised her fist. One quick rap. Nothing. Another. Still nothing.

Maggie knocked harder. The door swayed inward, whining loudly at the injustice of being disturbed at such an hour. Maggie's eyes widened. She licked her lips. "Lavena?"

No answer.

If she stepped inside, would Lavena be startled and shoot her or something? These acquaintances of Slade's weren't your typical neighbors. Maggie fidgeted with her jacket. She could almost hear the time ticking away as she stood there like a coward.

She crossed the threshold. The room was dark as pitch. "Lavena."

Maybe she wasn't home. Where in the world would a woman her age be at this hour?

Maggie felt for a light switch. She couldn't find anything on the wall near the door. She considered the lighting situation upstairs where the only source was a couple of table lamps, and moved carefully through the darkness in search of one.

Her foot hit something hard. Maggie grunted. Sofa leg. There had to be a lamp near the sofa. She felt across the upholstered cushions. Her fingers encountered a leg. Human. Covered in terry cloth.

Maggie froze. No one moved or screamed or anything. She needed light. Her pulse kicked into hyperspeed. She moved past the pair of human legs and found a table at that end of the sofa. Frantic, she felt across the top until she touched the base of the lamp. She twisted the switch. Light pooled on the table and floor and the sofa.

Lavena sat on the sofa, her head lolled to one side as if she'd fallen asleep. A small round hole in the middle of her forehead had leaked blood in bright crimson rivulets down her face.

Maggie covered her mouth with both hands to hold back the scream. Her stomach revolted, threatened to expel any contents.

Blood and brain matter were splattered over the back of the sofa.

Maggie stumbled back, bumped a chair and crumpled into the seat. She rocked back and forth until the urge to scream or puke subsided. The smell of blood and death penetrated deep into her lungs.

How had someone shot her without Maggie hearing it? Then she remembered the attack at the motel. There had been no gun blasts. The shooters had used silencers of some sort.

Her hand shaking, she reached out and touched the poor woman's throat. Her skin was still warm but there was no pulse. Fear zapped Maggie. Lavena hadn't been dead long.

Help. Maggie needed help. She forced herself up and half ran, half staggered to the door. Lavena's grandson lived in the flat next door. Outside, one hand against the wall for support, Maggie made her way to Ramondo's door. She knocked, loud. No answer. Fear tightened around her chest. She knocked again. Nothing.

She reached for the knob and gave it a twist. It opened without resistance. Inside, like Lavena's place, it was dark. Still.

"Ramondo?"

Silence echoed in the room.

She felt for a switch, didn't find one. Slowly, she found her way around the room by touch until she discovered a lamp. She twisted the switch and light glowed from beneath the shade. No body. Relief made her knees weak. The room was sparsely furnished, but all looked as it should be. No overturned furniture. Nothing broken. No blood. Clothes lay on the floor by the bed as if Ramondo had undressed in preparation for turning in, but the bed was empty, save the tousled covers.

"Ramondo?" The flat was one big room and a bathroom, like the others. She pushed the bathroom door inward and flipped on the overhead light. Empty.

Maggie turned to go, but hesitated. That overwhelm-

ing feeling of dread started deep in her belly. She inhaled deeply, analyzed the smell.

Blood. Death.

Shaking, Maggie faced the tiny bathroom once more
and crossed to the tub. Her hand shaking, she drew back
the shower curtain.

Ramondo lay naked in the tub, a bullet hole in his
left temple.

Maggie backed out of the room. The urge to scream
didn't come this time. She shook so hard she could
scarcely put one foot in front of the other to get to the
front door.

She needed a phone. Gathering her courage, she
searched the flat. No landline. Her stomach roiling,
she turned to where Ramondo's discarded clothes lay.
She forced herself to rummage through his shirt and
then his trousers. Her fingers closed around his cell
phone.

"Thank God."

Maggie pressed keys, opened and closed the phone
twice. She couldn't get past the security code. Toss-
ing aside the phone, she raced back to Lavena's flat. A
frantic hunt revealed the same. No landline. If Lavena
had a cell phone it was nowhere to be found.

Hysteria setting in, Maggie rushed to the next flat,
the one beyond Ramondo's. She banged on the door and
called out for help. No one answered. Taking the stairs
two at a time, she checked the other two upper flats.
Doors locked, lights out, no answer to her pleas.

She descended the stairs and wandered until she
stood in the middle of the street. She turned all the
way around. There was no one to help. No place to go.
What did she do now? She didn't speak the language.

She had no phone. There were no lights on in any of the buildings. If anyone was inside, they weren't going to come out and help her.

The distinct sound of a footfall on stone shattered the silence. Maggie whirled around. She looked one way, then the other.

Someone was there.

She'd heard them.

But she could see nothing except shadows and faint patches of light from the moon and the sole streetlamp at the end of the block.

She visually measured the distance between where she stood and Lavena's flat.

Then she ran.

Footfalls slammed against the cobblestone street behind her.

Whoever was out there was coming!

Maggie burst into the flat and shoved the door shut behind her. Her fingers fumbled with the lock. She jammed it into place just in time for something—a boot or body—to ram into the door.

She backed away. The slamming against the door shook it. A weapon. She needed a weapon. Half running, half stumbling, she rushed around the room. Yanked out a cabinet drawer and searched its offerings, then another and another. She encountered cold steel. She wrapped her fingers around the biggest knife in the drawer.

The wooden door splintered and a scream bolted from her throat.

There was no place to hide.

No back door.

No time to figure out how to get a window open.

She headed for the bathroom.

The front door burst inward as she slammed the bathroom door shut and locked it.

Boot heels echoed on the tile floor just outside the bathroom door.

Like the bathroom upstairs, this one had no window, no escape.

The intruder bumped against the bathroom door and Maggie held out the knife in front of her. She tried to slow her breathing, to calm down. She had to be prepared to fight or she would end up dead just like Lavena and her grandson.

Her baby. Dear God, she hadn't protected her baby.

Agony swelled so swiftly that spots floated in front of her eyes.

No. She grabbed back control. She had to be strong.

The door splintered menacingly, allowing the lock to give way. The door flew open and a man filled the doorway, the weapon he'd obviously already used to murder two people in his hand.

Maggie went ice-cold.

He leveled the barrel of the weapon on her and said something in Spanish. She didn't get a word of it.

Shaking so hard she could scarcely remain vertical, Maggie waved the knife. "Don't come any closer," she warned, her voice so keen and thin it was alien to her ears.

He took a step toward her.

She braced for the worst.

"Drop the knife," he said in English.

She blinked at the abrupt change in language, then told herself to focus, pay attention. No way was she doing anything he said.

She backed up a step and hit the side of the tub.

Another boot length disappeared between them.

The ice that had filled Maggie's limbs leached into her skull. The fear and panic drained away. She felt nothing except determination.

She would not let this bastard kill her baby.

He took the final step.She charged him and sank the knife into his shoulder.

He roared a string of curses and tried to grab her with his free hand. She kicked. Screamed. Stabbed at him with the knife.

When the gun clattered to the floor, Maggie rushed past him.

She was at the front door before he started running after her. Hope bloomed in her chest. If she could out-maneuver him, she could hide in the darkness.

Across the street she headed for a narrow alley. She ran as hard as she could, the bloody knife still clutched in her hand.

Laughter bubbled up into her throat. Hysteria was overtaking her. She struggled to tamp it down. *Keep running, Maggie. Don't slow down. Don't look back.*

He was getting closer. She could hear him coming.

She pushed herself harder. Ignored the sharp pain in her side. If she let him catch her…

Ruthless fingers tangled in her hair. Jerked her backward and off her feet.

She hit the unforgiving cobblestone.

The knife flew from her hand, bounced on the stone, landing somewhere out of her reach.

The world spun wildly as the spots reappeared, obscuring her vision. *Don't pass out!*

Looming over her, the man jammed the muzzle of

the gun against her forehead. He growled something crude in Spanish, his teeth clenched in fury. It was too dark to see his face well and she didn't understand the language, but she fully recognized his intent. He was as mad as hell and she was as good as dead.

"That's enough."

Maggie's mind scrambled to grasp where the voice had come from. Another man had followed them into the alley. The idea that they might have another horror planned for her exploded in her chest. *Please, God, don't let them do unspeakable things to me before they kill me.*

The first man bored the muzzle a little deeper into her skin and spat more ugly words she couldn't understand.

"Enough," the other man repeated. "Get her up."

Before the words could fully penetrate the terror swaddling her brain, the man with the gun had hauled her to her feet.

The second man waited a few feet away. He looked American and spoke English with no distinguishable accent. Unlike the man manacling her who wore jeans and a T-shirt, the one who seemed to be in charge wore a suit. He smiled at Maggie.

To his comrade, he said, "We need her alive and undamaged." His attention fixed on Maggie once more. "For now."

Chapter Eleven

4:00 a.m.

Slade parked the borrowed Jeep in a gulley below the rise overlooking the expanse of rugged terrain that separated his position from the Marek compound. She would be expecting him. The key was to breach the secure perimeter before she was aware of his imminent presence. Not an easy feat. But not impossible.

He adjusted his night-vision goggles and surveyed the stone wall that rose a full twelve feet high all the way around the main house, wrapping it with a menacing facade guaranteed to deter. He counted the usual three perimeter guards. No, wait, there was a fourth man. Slade tracked the man's progress as he made his rounds.

She was definitely expecting company.

Security would be on high alert.

There would be at least four more men inside. Various trip-wire and spring-activated traps in the outer perimeter. Motion-activated cameras strategically placed around the wall as well as inside the compound. He'd faced similar challenges many times. It wasn't the getting in that was the real issue.

Getting out without neutralizing the entire security force as well as the woman in charge would be unmanageable in the best-case scenario. He lowered the goggles. He was prepared for that risk.

He'd lived dozens of lives, leaving each one behind like a dead soul, not quite real enough or dead enough to matter in the scheme of things. This time might be his last, but he wasn't going alone. *She* was going with him. Straight to hell, if he had anything to say about it.

No more waiting. He wanted to be inside before sunrise.

He alternately slid and climbed back down to the Jeep. Mentally, this final confrontation had been coming for a long time. He was ready. Physically, he'd taken the usual preparatory steps. During his last shower he had not used soap or shampoo, and no deodorant. He didn't want the enemy to smell him coming. She recruited and trained her own security staff. No detail would be left to chance. His shoes had soft leather soles to ensure noiseless movements and his outerwear was black, made of a fabric that created no sound when it rubbed against other materials.

Outside of blowing up the place—and that was out of the question since Alayna was likely inside—this was the best he could do to ensure success.

His cell vibrated. He reached into the pocket of his ammo vest, his own internal alert moving to the next level. Only one person had this number besides Alayna. If Maggie was calling, that meant there was trouble back in Mexico City. In that event, he was too far away to help. Unknown Number flashed on the screen. The unfamiliar sting of fear trickled into his veins.

He slid the phone open, accepting the call, and waited.

"Tripp, you must listen closely. I don't have much time."

Alayna.

She was the one person who called him by that name without eliciting fury.

"I'm listening." There was always the chance that the Dragon would attempt to set him up. She would use any means to get to him. Nothing was beneath her. A computer re-creation of his sister's voice was certainly within the realm of possibility. But he knew his sister. She would never give up this number. Not even to avoid death. As much as the Dragon worshipped Alayna, she would execute her for that kind of betrayal if she learned of it. No question. Alayna was taking a huge risk calling him. She had taken many risks on his behalf over the years, but this was the greatest.

"Lavena and Ramondo are dead."

That foreign trickle of fear burst like a crack in a compromised dam, sending adrenaline gushing full force through him. "Maggie?"

"Two of her security team are bringing Maggie here." Alayna provided the route and their current position as well as the make of the vehicle. "Hurry, Tripp. If she reaches the compound…"

She didn't have to spell it out. The Dragon would torture Maggie mercilessly and she would use her to corner him. She thought she had gotten the jump on him. Slade cleared his mind. "I understand." He disconnected. Every second Alayna remained on the line was an additional risk. He had what he needed to intercept.

Slade tucked the phone away. Rage simmered deep

in his gut. The Dragon had finally gotten Lavena. Ramondo, too. The stakes were set. The Dragon wanted him terminated this time as much as he wanted her dead. There would be no attempts at negotiation as there had been in the past. No surprise, really.

This was the endgame.

He would not allow Maggie to be collateral damage. The Dragon had already taken far too much from him.

6:05 a.m.

MAGGIE HAD LOST ALL TRACK of time. The black bag that had been placed over her head prevented her from seeing anything at all. One of the men had tossed her into the cargo area of an SUV just before tying her up and covering her head. Her pitiful attempts to fight him off had done nothing but made him laugh. She had no idea in which direction they had gone, and accurately measuring the passage of time was impossible. The road had grown bumpier after that last turn, but she had no idea if that meant they were nearing their destination or simply taking a lot of back roads.

She had cried silently at first. Mostly for her baby. These men were taking her to that evil woman—Slade's mother. No doubt she wanted to use Maggie to lure Slade to her. The two captors hadn't said as much but she knew. There was no other reason to allow her to live. Maggie would be just as dead as Lavena and Ramondo if there wasn't a need to keep her alive.

Images of their lifeless bodies kept bobbing to the surface of the confusion, fear and exhaustion whirling in her head. Maggie tried to keep the images at bay, but she no longer had the fortitude to keep up the effort.

The bindings around her wrists had cut into her flesh. She'd tried for what felt like forever to wiggle her hands loose. All she had succeeded in doing was chafing her already raw skin even worse. Her feet hadn't been bound. She supposed they weren't afraid of her running if the opportunity presented itself, when she couldn't see where she was going.

She squeezed her eyes shut and prayed again for her life to be spared so her baby would be safe. Each time she prayed, she asked for Slade's protection, as well. What this evil woman had put him through as a child was unspeakable. She didn't deserve to live. What kind of woman did such horrific things to her child? Slaughtered an old woman and her grandson, and no telling how many others?

Slade had warned Maggie that she couldn't possibly comprehend and she now knew for a certainty that he was all too right. This was far beyond her scope of comprehension. She would never be able to assimilate such a tragedy.

If she had only been able to get to a phone before these scumbags had arrived, she could have called the Colby Agency for help. If anyone had the ability to help her and Slade, Victoria and Lucas did. But it was too late for that now. Their chances of rescue were a big fat zero.

Maggie's family would be devastated. She had told them a little about Slade. Each time she'd visited for holidays he had been too busy to go. Always an excuse. Her sisters had gotten a little suspicious in the last couple of months. Maggie had insisted everything was fine. She had lied to herself and to them.

Her family would be forced to suffer this nightmare

all because Maggie had been too blind to see. The positive pregnancy tests would be found in the bathroom of her apartment, giving her family an additional lost life to mourn. That would be the most devastating blow of all. Her sisters, with whom she shared everything, would be hurt that she hadn't told them. If only there had been time… She wanted so desperately to share that wondrous news with her family.

And with Slade. But she wasn't at all sure if that was the right decision. Too much had happened to explore the concept as she should have.

The SUV slowed. Maggie's heart seemed to pound hard enough to crack her ribs. The men spoke in Spanish, though she knew both spoke English, as well. Apparently they had recognized that she couldn't understand the language and wanted to ensure she was kept off guard. She listened intently, tried to pick up on a word here and there.

Gas. She was pretty sure she heard something about gas or gasoline. As if to confirm her assessment, the vehicle rolled to a stop. A door opened, then slammed shut. Then another opened and closed.

The urge to act swam in her brain. If they were at a gas station, was there anyone out there to hear her if she screamed? What time was it?

The cargo door opened, the shift in the air made her breath catch. Something hard nudged her head. "Make a sound and I will ensure you regret it."

Anger roared. "What're you going to do? Kill me? I don't think so." She braced to push upright, but the muzzle jammed into her skull hard enough to leave a mark. She ignored it, tried to sit up.

"There are far worse things than death, lady. Don't make me prove my point."

Her anger wilted like a pansy in the hot summer sun. As much as she wanted to take the risk and scream at the top of her lungs, she couldn't. She had no way of knowing if anyone was outside to hear her. Protecting the baby had to be her first priority.

The vehicle shifted with the weight of first one, then the second man getting back into the SUV. Doors slammed and the engine started. Her flimsy hope of rescue died an instantaneous death.

Defeat crushed down on her. *No. Stop it.* She would not think that way. As long as she was breathing there was hope. To distract herself, she pondered baby names. For a girl, Madelyn like her mother. That was a given. For a boy, maybe…Slade? But she didn't know if that was his real name. He'd mentioned something about using lots of different names. Was Slade a name he liked since he had chosen it? Would naming a son after him be smart since he wouldn't be a part of their lives?

Look at the facts, Maggie. Slade, the only name she knew him by, was the father of this child. Every aspect of him that she had fallen in love with was what made him Slade Keaton to her. She certainly wasn't going to tell her child that his father had been…a killer and yet somehow a protector. A ruthless man who had burrowed his way into her life to get close to the Colby Agency for reasons she still didn't understand.

No. She would tell her child about the good she had seen in Slade. How he had helped the Colby Agency a couple of times. How he had made Maggie feel special as no one else ever had. Those were the things she would tell her child when the time came.

Maggie closed her eyes and thought of all the nursery rhymes her mother used to tell her and her sisters. And the ones she'd heard her sisters tell their children. She smiled as the singsong voices whispered through her mind. Whatever happened at the end of this journey, she wanted her last thoughts to be of home and family. Slade's image loomed amid the others.

Him, too. He would always be a part of her.

SLADE LAY IN THE DITCH AND waited. According to his calculations the SUV would be passing this position within the next three minutes. A rifle would have served this purpose better, but he didn't have that luxury. The handgun would have to do.

He'd hidden his Jeep well off the road behind an abandoned gas station. The cover it provided had been the determining factor in choosing this location. On this leg of the road there were little options for cover. He had been in place long enough for any dust his arrival had stirred to settle.

Sunrise was a full half hour away, but that would work to his advantage. He needed every possible advantage.

A sound tagged his attention. He cocked his head and listened. The distant roar of an engine warned that a vehicle approached from the west. It had to be them. This remote section of road had few travelers, particularly at this hour.

His muscles tensed in preparation for battle. The headlights came into view over a distant rise. His finger snugged against the trigger.

The SUV grew closer. Slade had to aim carefully. His guess was that Maggie would be restrained in the backseat or the cargo area. Keeping gunfire away from those areas was imperative.

Closer. *Don't act yet. Hold your position.*

He pulled the night-vision goggles into place and avoided looking directly at the headlights. The glare made wearing the goggles uncomfortable.

Closer.

He pressed the trigger, putting a bullet through the driver's window, hopefully into the bastard's head. The SUV swerved right. He took out the front driver's-side tire, then the rear tire on the same side. The SUV bumped over the rough terrain on the other side of the road, then jolted to a stop.

Slade moved. If the other guy had a chance to get behind the wheel, he would take off.

He rushed across the road, his dark clothing allowing him to move unseen.

Activity in the vehicle snagged his attention. He couldn't make out what was happening, but he felt confident the driver's sidekick was attempting to take control of the SUV.

A scream rent the air.

Maggie!

Slade ran harder.

A shot hit the ground next to him and he dived for the dirt and rolled.

More shots puffed in the air, the silenced weapon taking potshots at the threat the shooter couldn't quite see. These men were skilled marksmen. The darkness was all the advantage Slade had.

He crawled forward, moving quickly toward the opposite side of the vehicle.

A door slammed on the other side of the vehicle. Maggie screamed again.

He'd dragged her out of the SUV.

Damn.

Slade curled into a ball behind the rear driver's-side wheel. Maggie was pleading with the guy to let her go. Slade tuned out the fear in her voice.

"Come out where I can see you," the man shouted, "or I'll kill her."

Maggie cried out in pain.

Fury tightened Slade's jaw. His instincts told him that the guy wouldn't dare kill her. That he likely had very specific orders about Maggie. But assuming that the man wouldn't panic was a dicey approach.

Slade took the risk. "Let her go and I'll let you live."

His enemy laughed. "I've heard that from more than one man before he died."

Slade leaned past the wheel and fired a shot. He hit the gunman in the ankle thanks to the night-vision goggles. The next scream wasn't Maggie's.

Moving quickly, Slade rounded the vehicle and leveled a bead on the guy wrestling to keep Maggie from escaping.

Damn. She needed to be still.

The guy sensed Slade's presence, let go of Maggie and pulled off a shot. Slade fired back and dropped him in one shot. Maggie scrambled away.

"It's okay now," he assured her. He checked the man on the ground. He was dead. Slade pushed up the goggles and went to Maggie.

She screamed when he touched her. His chest ached at the sound. "It's okay. It's me." He untied the bag and pulled it from her head. She trembled. He helped her to her feet. "Hold on and I'll cut your hands free." He fished the knife from his pocket and carefully, using his fingers to check before sliding the blade between her skin and the ropes, cut the bindings. Dawn had broken but it was still damn dark.

Maggie swayed as she faced him, then dived into his arms. She sobbed against his shoulder. She whispered over and over that she'd been afraid he was dead.

He tucked her hair behind one ear and manufactured a smile, whether she could see it or not. "We have to get out of here."

She nodded her understanding.

"You injured?" He held her at arm's length and tried to check her for injury, but there wasn't enough light.

"I'm okay." She scrubbed her hands over her face, then pressed one to her stomach. "I'm okay."

She might not be injured, but she was far from okay. Slade shoved his weapon into his waistband and draped an arm around her shoulder to usher her forward. The sooner they were in that Jeep and out of here, the better.

A distinct hiss dislocated the silence. Hot metal sliced through his left biceps.

Slade pushed Maggie to the ground, simultaneously reaching for his weapon and whirling to face the threat. He fired into the SUV three times.

The report of his weapon echoed in the distance, then silence reigned once more.

No return fire. Moving cautiously, he approached the vehicle and peered inside. This time the driver was done. Slade swore. He should have checked after putting the other guy down. Another mistake. His arm burned like hell.

No time to deal with that right now.

Maggie was already back on her feet by the time he reached her.

She gasped at the tear in his sleeve that revealed the slash in his flesh.

"It's not as bad as it looks."

At the rate he was going, he wasn't going to live to take down the Dragon.

MAGGIE ALLOWED HIM TO USHER her away from the SUV. Her head spun with all the questions she wanted to ask. How had he found her? How had he learned that she had been abducted? Did he know about Lavena and Ramondo? She couldn't find her voice or the brainpower to put the questions into words.

He ushered her across the road and in the direction of a long-closed gas station. Dawn crept across the desert, garishly highlighting the boarded-up windows and graffiti of the abandoned business. Behind the building a Jeep waited.

Slade helped her into the passenger side of the Jeep, then climbed behind the wheel. "Do you need me to drive?" She'd finally stopped shaking. Her brain was attempting to function once more. He had to be in pain.

"I'm good."

She didn't argue with him. Even she recognized that putting as much distance as possible between them and here was imperative.

Maggie relaxed against the seat. Her wrists burned, but she didn't care. Slade had rescued her. Her baby was safe and he was alive.

And they were together.

But how long would that last?

She turned to him. The rising sun shone on his dark

hair and his beard-shadowed jaw. Her heart squeezed painfully. How would this end? If only he would let her call the Colby Agency...maybe they could help.

Only one way to find out. "We should take care of your arm."

"Eventually."

She glanced over the seat and noted the backpack. "No first aid supplies?"

He shook his head. "We'll stop farther down the road."

Maggie stared forward. She bit her lip and dredged deep for courage. *Just do it.* "I believe the Colby Agency would be able to help us."

The silence that followed was not what she'd expected.

She gave him a little time to absorb the idea, then she added, "Victoria and Lucas have the best team. They work all sorts of cases."

More of that silence. Not a no, exactly. Just a no comment.

She spotted a building coming up on the right. Squinting hard, she made out the name on the sign. It appeared to be a convenience store and gas station. One that wasn't boarded up.

"We should stop and get something for your arm."

Without responding, he slowed and made the turn. When she reached for the door handle, he stopped her. "No phone calls."

Maggie nodded. For now. She would pursue that avenue again as soon as they were safe.

The word echoed in her head as she strode to the entrance of the convenience store. Would either of them ever be safe again?

She smiled for the clerk behind the counter. The girl was young. Seemed a heck of a place for a young girl to work. Way out here in the middle of nowhere. Maggie gathered what appeared to be peroxide, antibiotic ointment, over-the-counter pain medication and an array of bandages. They didn't have gauze or tape. On second thought, she grabbed a small package of feminine-hygiene pads and a couple of bandannas.

After placing the items on the counter, she produced another smile for the clerk. "Do you speak English?"

The girl nodded. "Yes. Can I help you?"

The urge to ask for a phone…to break down and tell someone how killers were chasing them stole Maggie's voice for a moment.

She cleared her throat. "This is peroxide? For cleaning a wound?"

"Yes."

They went through the other items to be sure Maggie had what she needed. At the last second she grabbed some bottled water and snacks. Before the clerk finished tallying up the bill, Maggie added two cups of coffee.

She carried the two brown paper bags to the Jeep and climbed in. Once she'd put the bags on the floorboard, she passed a coffee to Slade and cradled one for herself. It wasn't until that moment that she realized how cold she was. She was freezing.

Slade hit the road again before she could argue. "What about your arm?" She needed to bandage it up at the very least.

"We'll get to that."

She knew better than to try to change his mind.

"Where are we going?" She was utterly lost. Being

blindfolded hadn't helped, but since she'd never been to Mexico before she knew nothing about the area.

"Someplace I hope they won't find you."

That he wanted to hide her away again so he could go off like a lone wolf to complete his quest irritated her. He still hadn't answered her question about calling the Colby Agency. "Why can't we get help?" It made total sense to her. As evil as his mother was, she wasn't invincible. Just because she had escaped the law so far didn't mean she would forever.

"I explained the answer to that question already. They can't help us. No one can." He didn't meet her eyes, just kept his attention fully on driving.

Maggie refused to believe what he said.

Whether he agreed or not, first chance she got she was calling Victoria.

Chapter Twelve

7:45 a.m.

"What have you done?"

Alayna turned from the window to meet her mother's fierce glare. She had been expecting this confrontation for the last hour. Her brother had had time to intercept the men who had taken his woman. Apparently he had been successful.

"What's happened?" Alayna adopted an expression of innocence and surprise. "Is he here?" she added for good measure, infusing hope into her tone. Her mother was aware that she cared deeply for her brother.

Camille strode up to Alayna, her fury radiating in violent waves. "Siegel called to say they were ambushed en route. We've been unable to contact him since the initial call."

Alayna blinked as if confused. "Was it him?" She didn't dare say her brother's name out loud. It was forbidden.

"You have gone too far this time, Alayna." Camille moved her head slowly from side to side. "All these years I have trusted you. I have given you everything. And you allowed me to believe that you remained steadfast and loyal. But I now know that you were keeping much from me." She lifted her chin in resolution. "I've just been informed that you have betrayed me time and time again."

Alayna struggled to keep the panic from her voice. "I don't understand." Fear wrapped around and around her throat, tightening like a snake determined to render its prey helpless before devouring it. How had she discovered what Alayna had been up to? She had been so cautious.

"You have kept him informed of our security measures. You," Camille accused, her lips tight with fury, "warned him of this morning's action. Your actions were deliberate and without excuse."

Like there was ever a good enough excuse for the Dragon. The trembling started in Alayna's bones. She labored fiercely to keep it in check. If her mother saw the depth of her fear she would know her accusations were true. "I have no idea how to contact him," she argued, trying to sound offended. "How could you think such a thing?" She reached out to her mother. "You know I am loyal to you. I always have been."

Camille drew away, disdain in her eyes. "The two of you were my greatest successes. When the others failed, you thrived. First he betrayed me, and now you." Her fingers curled into fists. "My only hope now lies with the younger ones. You are dead to me, Alayna."

Her mother wheeled and walked out of the room.

Alayna couldn't move. She held herself together until Camille was gone and the door closed. The shuddering took over then, weakening her knees until she had to brace herself against the nearest table to remain standing.

Despite the reality of what this meant, a faint smile

tugged at her trembling lips. Her brother had succeeded. His Maggie would be safe now. Alayna prayed her brother would take Maggie and disappear. He should never come back here. Never, ever.

But he would not run from the danger. Not this time. The end was near. For them all, Alayna feared.

The doors opened. Two guards stormed into the room, coming toe to toe with her.

"You are to come with us."

Alayna stared at the man who had spoken. Eli Kennemore, Camille's chief of security, had not said her name. Defeat settled on her shoulders. In the face of that foreboding weight, she affirmed her ground, shoulders back, chin lifted in defiance. She would die with dignity.

"How dare you address me in such a way." She noted the glint of uncertainty in his eyes and garnered some satisfaction from that small victory.

"I have my orders," Eli maintained. "You must come with us."

Alayna snubbed her own rising uncertainty. With all that she knew, a part of her still needed confirmation. "Say my name."

The man she had known since she was a child stared at her now, regret written plainly on his face. "It is forbidden."

And so it was as her mother said. Alayna was dead.

She pushed between the two men and exited the room. Her heart pounded, sending the blood roaring through her brain.

Resignation filled her, strangely heralding a sense of welcome relief. Her brother had suffered enough. If her life was the cost of his freedom, Alayna was happy to pay the price.

CAMILLE PACED HER ROOM. How could Alayna do this to her? She paused to stare at the monitors that kept her abreast of ongoing operations and world events. Everything was right on schedule. She was a master. Whatever operations she undertook were always a success. And no one had ever seen her coming or going. Camille had learned a long time ago that many layers were necessary to survive in this business. Every aspect of her operation was layered in such a way that years of research would be required to narrow down a specific detail. By that time she would have changed all of it.

That was the other important factor. Change.

But she had not been able to protect against the human emotion element.

How could her own progeny betray her? The first two were nothing more than mistakes. With *him* she had miscalculated certain variables. His biological father had been burdened with that same extreme sense of self-righteousness. Until that genetic defect had surfaced, Tripp Marek—even thinking his name sickened her—had been the perfect operative. Unstoppable.

But he had turned. The possibility that he had inherited that defective gene from his aunt infuriated Camille. Lavena had been a fool. Camille had offered to take care of the stupid old woman after her husband died fifteen years ago. She had been too full of that holier-than-thou rubbish, as well. She would starve, she'd claimed, before she would take a dime from Camille.

All these years Camille had tolerated her insolence. She had shown far too much mercy merely because Lavena had taken care of her as a child after the loss of their parents. Lavena had defied her on every front. Crossed her at every opportunity.

No more. She had gotten what she deserved just as her no-good grandson had.

Camille felt no regret at having ordered her older sister's death. She showed allegiance to no one but herself. Cared for no one...except Alayna.

Now she was gone, too.

No. Not now. Alayna had been betraying her for many years. Slipping information to her brother to protect him. Her biological father had been a cold-blooded assassin. She should not have inherited such weaknesses. Clearly, her brother's behavior had influenced her.

He would pay for his betrayal. Rage detonated inside Camille. He would pay even more dearly for taking Alayna from her. The Code was broken, the prototype a failure. But there were more coming, almost ready. Six expertly trained to begin a new program. Near-perfect assassins and relentless infiltrators. Nothing would stop her this time. She had learned a hard lesson with the first group. That group had been four in number, all born of her body. Not one had inherited her unmatched abilities.

Being biologically involved had been a mistake, putting her at a disadvantage in terms of recognizing a weakness before the defect grew out of control. The surrogates for this new Code had been disposed of immediately after birth, breaking that infernal biological bond before it could become an obstacle.

Camille lingered a moment, staring out the window at the fertile landscape she prized so highly. The land was the one thing in this life she could trust. It remained steadfast.

Unlike him.

For his betrayal, the punishment had to fit the crime. She wanted her last remaining son to writhe in agony and gnash his teeth.

Physical pain would not be sufficient. She had trained him too well.

Camille smiled. The answer was utterly simple.

First, she would slowly torture this redhead he seemed to need to protect. How dare he show such weakness by allowing a woman so close. For her part in his fall, she would die first. Death would come to this pathetic creature in tiny increments. But the coup de grâce would be even more shattering.

Lucas Camp and his beloved wife had revealed Alayna. Had they not interfered, perhaps Alayna would not have taken this final step of betrayal. Like Maggie James, Lucas would die, equally slowly. Starting with his one good leg perchance. Camille laughed. Oh, yes, she would have the esteemed Lucas Camp dismantled one limb at a time, then one organ at a time. Until the last drop of his self-righteous blood had leaked from his cold, lifeless body.

Maybe she would video the entire procedure and send it to his lovely widow.

Perfect.

Camille would lose much this day, but the final, lethal blow would be hers. Perhaps this would be her greatest achievement yet.

Chapter Thirteen

Colby Agency, Chicago, 8:00 a.m.

"The jet is ready."

Victoria turned from her treasured window. Whenever her world was a little shaky she could count on the view of the city she loved to steady her.

"Excellent," she said to her husband. She needed every ounce of strength she possessed right now. "I'm ready."

Lucas did not want her to go. But how could she not? Every instinct she possessed warned that this was somehow as much about Lucas as it was about Slade Keaton.

"I wish you'd change your mind."

The worry etched in Lucas's face tugged at her heartstrings. He was exhausted. They had both been up all night. Ian Michaels had confirmed that Keaton and Maggie had left the country. The pilot who'd returned to Chicago last evening had happily given all the details as soon as Simon Ruhl had called in his friend from the Federal Bureau of Investigation. Jim had left for Mexico City immediately upon hearing the news. The agency's jet had returned only a few hours ago.

After a much-needed rest and necessary preparations, the agency's pilot was prepared to return to Mexico City with Victoria, Lucas and Ian. Simon would stay behind and coordinate activities here. Thomas Casey, Lucas's dear friend from the CIA, continued to liaise with Lucas as well as with Interpol.

The Dragon was wanted in several countries. If she was found, treason charges would be the least of her worries. Victoria suspected that whatever punishment she received would not be nearly severe enough.

Lucas joined Victoria at the window, and he cupped her face in his hands. "At least four people are dead already. I don't want you any closer to the fire than you already are. I could not bear it if you were hurt any more so than you already have been."

Two deceased assassins had been discovered at the motel near the major interstate between Chicago and St. Louis. A truck driver's conscience had gotten the better of him hours after the incident and he'd called the police. Chicago P.D. had informed Jim of what they knew. After sitting in on the interview with the pilot who had taken Maggie and Keaton out of the country, Jim had headed for Mexico. From the airfield outside Mexico City he had traced Keaton's movements to a borough called Coyoacán. Two more victims had been discovered. The collateral damage was piling up. Victoria and her agency had to do something. Maggie was an innocent in all this. Victoria speculated that on some level Keaton was, as well.

Lucas did not agree. But they both concurred that action had to be taken.

Victoria offered her husband a smile. "Whatever happens, Lucas, I will be at your side."

He sighed, the sound weary and filled with worry. "You are far too courageous for your own good."

Victoria pressed a kiss to his lips. "I belong at your side, for better or worse." She draped her arms around his waist and pulled him close. "Besides, we both owe it to Maggie to do all we can. Her family and friends are worried sick. We have to bring her safely home." Victoria had made that promise to Maggie's older sister, and she would not break that vow. "Don't ask me to ignore what I feel. This is something I must do, Lucas. It's far too important to all of us."

"This may not turn out the way we hope." Lucas had warned her repeatedly that this evil Dragon was by far the deadliest enemy either of them had faced thus far. "She won't be easy to defeat. Not even with all our resources."

"We won't be defeated." Victoria refused to consider that option. Good would prevail over this heinous woman. To believe otherwise was too unthinkable.

"If there's no dissuading you…" Lucas relented. His arms went around her and held her close. "But I want you in the background."

Victoria pressed her cheek to his chest. She loved listening to the beat of his heart. They had talked about his brief relationship with this woman who called herself the Dragon. He had been drawn to her because she reminded him so much of Victoria. At the time, Victoria had been married to James. Lucas had been in love with her even then, but Victoria hadn't known. Maybe she'd sensed he had deep feelings for her, but she had been so in love with her first husband and the father of her only child that she had dismissed the idea.

That Lucas had loved her for all those years, had waited selflessly, made her love him all the more.

Victoria lifted her gaze to meet his. "We have to try to protect Keaton, as well. You must see that."

Her husband's expression darkened. "He brought this to us. Put you in danger at least twice—"

"We can't prove that he was responsible for any of those events. You know that." Victoria was convinced that Keaton had simply been watching so closely that he'd picked up on trouble before anyone else. Watching her and Lucas had been his singular focus. "Until we understand what brought him here and how that plays into what's happening now, we have an obligation to help him."

"He has put you in danger, Victoria." Lucas spoke sternly. "And he may cost Maggie her life. You can't view this any other way. He is dangerous to anyone around him simply by virtue of his connection to the Dragon. That is what we do know."

"Lucas." Victoria had broached this subject already, but the escalating events had prevented her from pursuing the idea. "You have to seriously consider that Slade Keaton may be your son." Lucas had no children of his own, unless Slade Keaton proved to be his biological child. But her husband had loved Victoria's son just as much as if he'd been his own. He loved their grandchildren. Lucas was not a man who could do otherwise.

He looked away a moment, the concept clearly too painful to bear. "Why would she have kept a secret like that from me? Wouldn't she have wanted to use that information to her advantage? There were numerous opportunities when I was involved in high-level operations with the capacity for worldwide ramifications. We are talking about a woman deeply entrenched in the world of intelligence."

He had a valid point. Victoria considered that view for a moment. Then she understood the motive, and conviction flooded her on the heels of the epiphany.

A rap on the door of her office drew their attention there. Ian waited in the open doorway. "We're ready to depart."

"On our way," Lucas assured him.

Victoria surveyed her office one last time as she gathered her purse and scarf. She glanced out the window and said a quick prayer that they would all make it back here safely.

Lucas helped her into her jacket and escorted her to the elevators. As they waited for one to arrive, Victoria needed to finish what she'd had to say before Ian's arrival.

"Lucas." He turned to her. "I think you're right about her using Keaton to her advantage. I think she has likely done that his entire life." She searched her husband's eyes. "But I think there's something else she has considered more advantageous and that's why you never knew. She had an ace up her sleeve if she ever needed one. The precise opportunity just hadn't presented itself."

Lucas slowly nodded. "I've considered that possibility myself. Thomas is looking into what she's been up to. But uncovering her secrets won't be easy. She's a master at concealment."

A soft chime announced the elevator's arrival. Victoria took her husband's hand and squeezed it. "I think we're about to find out what she's been up to."

Chapter Fourteen

8:48 a.m.

Slade had driven around for more than an hour before choosing this primitive village. Maggie couldn't even pronounce the name, much less spell it. He'd rented an abandoned shack on the outskirts of the village from an old man who claimed to own it. There was no electricity or plumbing. A ragged bed leaned in one corner of the single room, while a scarred, wobbly table surrounded by two worn chairs huddled in the center. The cracks in the floorboards were wide enough for every manner of insect and rodent to feel welcome. Two windows were nothing more than square holes in the battered walls. Cobwebs lined most corners while dust coated every flat surface.

After what she'd been through, luxury wasn't high on her priority list. She could live with candles and bottled water.

What she couldn't live with was Slade's insistence on getting himself killed. He still intended to go after the Dragon while leaving Maggie here, alone, in this remote village. Like last time, he'd gathered supplies from a local general store of sorts. She sensed the urgency in his every move.

She desperately wanted to call for help. Did they even have telephone service here? Slade kept his cell phone in his vest pocket. Her chances of getting her hands on it were about negative ten.

He refused to listen to reason! Couldn't he see that they needed help?

"Can I have a look at your arm now?" The bleeding had stopped, but he hadn't taken the time to allow her to clean the wound or bandage it.

He moved from the window and sat down in one of the chairs. "Sure."

Maggie had no idea what had happened between the time he left her at the flat and when he'd ambushed her kidnappers, but he seemed more remote than usual. She picked through the bags of supplies she'd gotten at the store. No need for the feminine-hygiene pads now since the bleeding had stopped. She'd had the fleeting idea since some guy patronizing her coffee shop who'd gotten a terrible nosebleed had used one of his girlfriend's tampons to staunch the flow. The peroxide, ointment and bandages she could use. And the bandannas. Who knew how clean they were. She'd chosen a pale blue, the lightest color available, in hopes that the residual dye in the fabric would be minimal.

"Do you want to take off your shirt?" The sleeves were long and there was the vest over the shirt. She bit her lower lip as she considered having the opportunity to get her hands on that cell phone tucked in one those vest pockets. Service might be nonexistent here, but she would sure like the chance to try.

He stood, peeled off the black vest with all its pockets and gear, then he tugged the skintight shirt over his head. He grimaced as the sleeve rolled off his injured arm. Maggie winced on his behalf. That had to hurt.

As soon as he was seated again, she inspected the wound. An ugly tear, shallow enough not to have hit bone. She didn't know about muscle damage. What they really needed was a doctor.

"You might need stitches." She frowned at the bloody, angry gash.

"Clean it up and bandage it with whatever you have." He glanced up at her. "Or I can do it."

She resisted the temptation to roll her eyes. "I'll do it. But if you get an infection, don't blame me."

He said nothing. She wasn't thick skulled. She realized that the injury was the least of his worries just now. A wave of weakness softened her knees. What in the world were they going to do?

Be strong, Maggie. He'd protected her so far. But she feared his ability to protect himself was sorely compromised. And that poor woman and her grandson. Slade hadn't said a word about them.

"I'm sorry about your friends." She cleaned away the blood from the injury, which took some doing. He didn't flinch. Didn't respond to her comment.

"Lavena seemed fond of you." Maggie had no idea what the dynamics of their relationship had been, but such heinous murders were a terrible thing just the same.

"She was a contact." He shifted in his chair as Maggie applied the ointment. "A resource. Nothing more."

Maggie considered his tone, the words he had used. "Whatever she was to you, she's dead now." It made her angry that he showed no sadness whatsoever. "Those terrible men shot her in her own house. They murdered her grandson in his bathtub. It was awful, just awful." Her voice grew more high-pitched as she spoke. She hadn't wanted to sound harsh, but she just couldn't ignore the truth as he seemed able to do.

"They knew the risks."

Maggie's hands fell away from his arm, her mouth gaped in astonishment. Just when she thought nothing else could shock her. "Did you hear yourself?" What kind of person thought like that?

The man to whom she had given her heart, apparently.

Slade looked up at her. "Did *you* hear me?"

What the Sam Hill did that mean? "I heard exactly what you said." She planted her hands on her hips and glared at him. How could he be so callous?

She couldn't do this. He grabbed her arm before she could turn away. He didn't speak until she looked at him. "I told you, you wouldn't like my world. This—" he pressed her with those dark gray eyes "—is my world. Kill or be killed. Walking away from the dead and just being glad it wasn't you."

Yanking her hand free of his, she tore at the wrappers on the bandages. Her fingers fumbled and that made her even madder.

"I'm not that man you imagined me to be," he went on. "I let you see what I wanted you to see. The rest you made up as we went along. That's what humans do. They fill in the blanks with the story they want to believe. You created the fairy tale, Maggie. I just gave you the jumping-off point."

Outrage burst inside her. "I made it up? Humans do this?" What did that make him? She slapped a palm against her chest. "I have the problem, is that it?" She couldn't believe this. Did he not see how wrong his thinking was? How could anyone so smart be so blind?

He reached for the bandages. "I knew you wouldn't understand."

Maggie stilled. Her insides went deathly quiet. It wasn't so much the words he said but the way he said them. Here was a man who had been abused, forced as a child to learn and accomplish horrific deeds most adults never experienced. His emotions had been battered out of him. He had carried that ugliness with him for thirty years. Most likely for the first time in all those years he had dared to share some part of that truth with someone and she had just done what he had feared all along.

She hadn't understood. She'd treated him like a freak.

He was undeniably correct. She was the one with the problem.

"I'm sorry. You're right." He didn't look at her as she spoke. "I'm the one with the problem." She watched as he fumbled with the bandages. Finally she couldn't take it anymore and pushed his hands away. "Let me do it."

Maggie took her time, lining up the bandages until the gash was fully covered. He definitely needed a few stitches, but there was not a thing she could do about that. Carefully, she wrapped a bandanna around the row of bandages and tied it snugly. "Maybe that'll work."

He glanced at his arm. "Thanks."

She washed her hands with the peroxide and the other bandanna. "You want something to eat?" There was a variety of snacks and bottled water. The way her stomach felt right now, she might not be able to keep anything down. "You must be starving."

He stood. "I don't need your sympathy."

Ire stirred once more as he strode to the window and stared out at the miles and miles of nothing but dirt and scrub grass. He wasn't going to make this easy. She had learned that when he wanted to push her away he avoided using her name. What was that all about? Was it because he'd changed identities so many times that names were somehow irrelevant?

Had he acquired an innate ability not to get attached to a name because he knew he would have to change it the next time that evil woman caught up with him? What kind of life was that?

"What's your real name?" Maggie asked as she joined him at the primitive window. The bright sun made her squint; looking at him made her yearn to touch that incredibly well-defined chest. It was crazy that even after what they'd been through and what she now knew, she was drawn to him on every imaginative level. Hormones? That had to be it. She forced herself to focus on her original question. "What was the name you were given at birth?"

"The names I've used in the past are irrelevant."

Since he didn't look at her and his tone was devoid of emotion, she wasn't sure if he meant what he said or if he just made the statement for the shock value. He'd proven consistent in his determination not to reveal any facts about himself, much less any emotions. That he'd shared anything personal was stunning. Then again, she figured that he had reason to believe she wouldn't survive this ordeal, or he wouldn't have given her that bit of information.

"But your birth name was different," she countered, unwilling to give up the fight for more. "That's your *true* name." He couldn't argue her point. Well, unless a person legally changed his or her birth name. She felt confident that wasn't the case.

He turned his head so that he stared down his shoulder at her. She knew that move. Intimidation. Subtle, but there nonetheless. That he towered over her, bare chested and looking incredibly sexy and somehow vulnerable at the same time, made her ache to reach out. But he didn't want her to touch him that way. He didn't want to connect on an emotional level, and the way she wanted to touch him was all about emotions.

"What difference does it make? I've told you too much already." His attention shifted back to the wide-open world outside where an ominous threat waited for him to show up for the final battle.

The big, wide world where he had never been safe, not a day in his life. Maggie ached at the thought. "It matters because it's yours," she said softly, her own emotion choking her. "No one but you has the right to take it away or discard it."

"I discarded it."

How could he be so detached about his identity? Who he was mattered. *He* mattered.

"If you discarded it that means you don't care, so why not tell me?" There. Let him come up with an excuse not to answer her now.

Rather than answer, he walked away from her.

Maggie almost gave up. What difference did it make? By tomorrow he would likely be dead or someplace else with a new name. Either way he would be gone.

If she survived, her child would grow up never knowing his father. Considering all that she knew, wouldn't that be a blessing?

Uncertainty tore at her. How was she supposed to know?

She should just tell him. The thought startled her. Her intention had been not to tell him. If he stayed because of the baby, that would be wrong. She wanted him to stay because he wanted to stay. Was that selfish of her? Should she be thinking of her child rather than herself? Would her child resent that she had withheld this truth from his father? It wasn't as if she would lie if her child asked one day.

And what about Slade? Didn't he have any rights? Wasn't that the reason he carried such a massive grudge? Because his own mother had never cared about his rights or his feelings?

Maggie summoned her shaky courage. "There's something you should know."

He dragged on his shirt. Reached for his vest.

"I'm serious, Slade." She almost laughed at herself. As if the past twenty-four hours or so had been anything other than serious.

"Stay inside. Away from the windows."

He wasn't going to answer her. He was leaving again. "You're leaving? After all that's happened?" She threw up her hands in frustration. "This suicide mission of yours is the biggest thing you've got going on?"

Her breath caught. She hadn't meant to say that.

For a single second he only stared at her. "I'll get word to you when it's safe to leave. If you don't hear anything, after forty-eight hours, call your friends at the Colby Agency. The old man who let this place can get you to a phone."

Maggie felt cold. Empty. But she knew what she had to do. "I'm pregnant."

He walked out the door.

SLADE KEPT WALKING. HIS instincts were railing at him to pay attention to his surroundings, but he couldn't do it. Her words kept ringing in his ears.

I'm pregnant.

He didn't have to ask her if she was certain. Maggie would know for sure before hitting him with this. She would never do this to trap him. She would never try to use anyone. Not him. Not a child.

His feet stalled, unable to continue carrying him wherever the hell he was going.

She had been carrying this burden since she'd shown up at the brownstone the night of the explosion. Had she come to tell him?

How could he be a father?

Fear twisted deep in his belly.

He couldn't be a father. He lacked the skills.

Didn't she know that he was incapable of true emotion? That he was nothing?

Movement on the narrow lane that led to the village dragged his attention back to the present. A man on a bicycle was…heading this way…shouting.

Slade's right hand went automatically to his weapon.

The man was still shouting when he braked to a stop so fast he almost landed in the dirt right in front of Slade. It was the old man who'd rented them this damn shack.

"Gringos in the village asking about you and the woman." He burst into Spanish from there.

Three men in a big black SUV were questioning villagers about Slade and the woman with red hair.

Slade glanced back at the window where Maggie watched.

She carried his child.

He had to protect her…had to protect that child…the way his father had not protected him.

Slade turned back to the old man still frantically waving his arms and rambling on about the gringos. Slade grabbed his wrist. When he had his full attention, he explained, "I have an offer for you."

The man's eyes widened with disbelief as Slade gave him the details. Two minutes later the old man drove away in the Jeep, headed back to the village. Slade rolled the bicycle back to the shack.

Maggie met him at the door. "I'm afraid to ask."

"They're in the village looking for us."

Her eyes rounded in fear as she stepped back to allow him to pass.

"I made a deal with the old man, but we have to lay low for a while." Slade gathered some of the snacks and a couple of bottles of water and tucked them into his backpack. Maggie stood right where he'd left her next to the door.

"That's it?"

She was angry. But this wasn't the time. He slung the backpack over his shoulder. "You did hear at least part of what the guy said, right?"

Without bothering to answer, she swiveled on her heel and walked out the door. Slade followed. He shook off the haze still cluttering his head. He'd deal with her news later.

If he lived long enough.

He swung onto the bike the old man had left. He patted the handlebars. "Hop up here."

She shot him an are-you-kidding look.

"I have no way to estimate how much time we have. I would suggest we get moving."

Maggie straddled the front wheel, braced her hands on the handlebars and hopped up. Slade licked his lips and resisted the urge to cup her backside with his hands. What was it about this woman that could, for a moment, make him forget even an impending threat?

Slade took the path the old man had told him about. He got to keep the Jeep if he convinced the gringos that the man and his redheaded woman had dumped it in favor of a better ride. The old man had no reason to renege on the deal. The Dragon's men wouldn't be offering any better deals. But Slade hadn't lived this long by assuming anything.

Rather than go to the cousin's house the old man had offered, Slade rode the bike to the rock outcropping a hundred or so yards from the shack and stopped. He set Maggie on her feet.

"Why are we stopping?"

"Just in case."

When the bike was hidden from view, Slade settled into position, binoculars and weapon in hand.

Maggie crouched down beside him. "Will they try to kill us now or take us to *her?*"

"As long as they don't find us, they won't do either." He scanned the road in both directions. The answer was far more complicated than that, but his comment would, hopefully, satisfy her.

Maggie hugged her arms around her knees. "Are you going to kill them?"

He lowered the binoculars. She was really worried. This type of maneuver was the norm for him. He had to remind himself that all of this was strange and terrifying to her. "If we're lucky, they'll check out the old man's story about us dumping the Jeep and leaving in another vehicle and move on."

"You'll let them drive away if they show up here?"

He nodded. "If they move on, that leaves us safe here."

Maggie pondered his explanation for a time. "We're staying here if they go?"

Slade met her expectant gaze. "If this goes down the way I want it to, you're staying here."

A moment of extended silence passed.

"You're still planning to go after her."

Not a question. Maggie was beginning to understand there was no other choice. He'd taken the only choice he'd had when he left twelve years ago. There would be no other choices as long as she was alive.

A cloud of dust announced the arrival of trouble well before Slade heard the engine. He lifted the binoculars and checked the passenger list. Three goons. The usual black SUV.

The SUV skidded to a stop in front of the shack. All three men piled out. One took the back, the others burst in through the front.

Slade lowered the binoculars and waited. The goons would find evidence of Maggie tending his wound. A couple of left-behind snacks and a half-empty bottle of water. He checked the time on his cell. Two minutes and they would be gone.

One of the men walked out of the shack and back to the SUV. He opened the cargo door at the rear of the vehicle.

Tension hardened Slade's muscles. This was not good.

The bastard dragged something from the SUV's cargo area.

The old man.
Damn.
They would kill him.

Chapter Fifteen

The air stilled. Maggie stopped breathing. The old man was begging for his life. She couldn't understand the words, but she fully comprehended the scene playing out in front of her.

He was going to die for helping her and Slade.

She looked to the man at her side. He wanted these men to leave with the impression that they were long gone. Was he really going to let that old man die to conceal their presence?

Did she want him to intervene and put their lives at greater risk? The baby's life at greater risk?

Two beats throbbed in her skull along with the screams echoing from below.

She couldn't sit here and let that old man die.

As if he'd read her mind, Slade fired a shot. The man taunting the old guy dropped to the ground before the blast stopped echoing in her ears.

The old man scrambled to get behind the SUV, scarcely evading the shots that peppered the ground around him. Bullets pinged off the rocks of their hiding place. The other two were shooting at them. The shot that had saved the old man had given away their presence and their position.

"Get down on the ground," Slade ordered.

She went facedown in the dirt, and her body started that now too-familiar shaking fueled by fear. Slade fired off three more shots before reaching into his backpack for a new clip. The old one hit the ground and the new one slid into the open slot.

Maggie's attention focused on his movements. Did he have enough ammunition to hold the two off? Was there anything she could do?

Panic welled so fast she couldn't breathe. He had been right about everything. She didn't understand his world. He reacted on instinct. The fundamental aspect of human emotions was obsolete in his world. How had he survived?

How were they going to survive now?

Even if they got through this time, what about the next? And the one after that? How could Slade win this battle? The Dragon's resources seemed endless.

He couldn't win. They couldn't win.

Maggie watched him alternate between ducking for cover and firing at the enemy. He remained completely focused, his movements smooth and unhesitating.

Trained to kill practically from birth.

No attachments. Not even to his own name.

How could he ever love her even if he wanted to? How could he love their child?

Maggie closed her eyes against the overwhelming sadness. As much as she feared dying, she felt both fear and regret for what he had suffered.

"You can get up now."

Maggie's eyes shot open. Her mind registered silence. No more bullets pinging around them. No more blasts from Slade's weapon cracking in the air. Then the old man was wailing again.

Slade grabbed his backpack and he stood. He offered his hand. Slowly, her movements unsteady, she pushed up, taking his hand for assistance.

He rolled the bike as she trudged along behind him, her gaze sweeping over the aftermath. The first man lay near the SUV. The second at the front corner of the shack. Number three lay halfway between the shack and the SUV. All head shots. All stone-cold dead.

Maggie hugged her arms around herself. She felt cold in spite of the sun bearing down on her. What on earth was she going to do?

Even if she survived and returned to her life, how would she ever put all this behind her? Her gaze settled on Slade. How would she put him behind her?

The old man from the village thanked Slade over and over for saving his life. Maggie watched, unable to react or think. She was past thinking. Her mind had shut down all but essential functions.

Slade and the old man spoke at length. Maggie didn't bother trying to translate.

When the old man had ridden away on his bike, she started to ask Slade what they were going to do, but he was checking the bodies. She tasted the bile rising in her throat. He removed their weapons and the extra clips in their pockets. After that he searched the SUV, found more ammunition clips and stored them in his backpack.

Finally he took her by the arm and guided her to the narrow path they'd started along before.

"Where are we going?" Some part of her brain was obviously still operating on autopilot, because she hadn't made a conscious decision to ask the question. The words just popped out.

"Back to the village."

THIRTY MINUTES WERE REQUIRED to walk back to the village via the winding path the old man named Rico had suggested. He had assured Slade that the cousin's house was vacant at the moment and that he would not betray him if anyone else came around asking, not even the police.

Slade felt confident the man's gratitude would keep him loyal.

A cleanup detail would come for the SUV and the bodies. It would be assumed that Maggie and he were long gone. That would buy the time Slade needed.

He knew full well what he had to do to protect Maggie and the child she carried. Leaving her tucked away would not be enough. The risk was too great.

Her words, and what those words meant, kept nagging at him. Later he'd have to analyze that meaning. Any distraction at this point could cost him any advantage they had gained.

The house belonging to Rico's cousin was a palace compared to the shack. A few narrow streets away from the center of the village, the houses were close and clean. There was plumbing and electricity. And food. Since Rico had arrived ahead of them, he had generously provided a few supplies.

"You look tired." Slade ushered Maggie into a chair. "I'll be outside for a minute."

She nodded but didn't question his intentions. That wasn't like Maggie at all. Worry gnawed at him.

Slade locked the front entrance and walked through

the house to the rear door. The yard was small and the neighbors close, but no one appeared to be home.

From the moment she had realized the seriousness of their situation, Maggie had wanted to call the Colby Agency. To Slade the idea had been out of the question. Though he no longer felt vindictive toward Lucas, Slade couldn't label what he did feel.

Two years ago he had swaggered into Chicago with a single goal. Get close to Lucas Camp and slowly but surely dismantle all that mattered to him. He'd started by purchasing the Equalizer shop from Victoria's son, Jim. That had positioned him strategically on a professional level. Then he had drawn Maggie into his treachery. She had provided the personal connection. He hadn't realized the potential at first. Her coffee shop had merely provided a tactical position. The rest had fallen into place by sheer coincidence.

The three months he had expected to spend on the mission had turned to six, then to a year. Suddenly two years had passed and he had become a part of the Colby clan. At first his curiosity about Lucas had drawn him, but, in time, it was Victoria who had lured him closer and closer. Though looking at her had been difficult at first, he had gotten over that obstacle. It wasn't like his *mother* had always looked like that. Lavena had shown him photos of the Dragon before. She had looked nothing like Victoria prior to setting her scheme in motion.

Slade hadn't asked the old woman how she happened to have the photos, but he had his suspicions. Just more irrelevant information, he had thought at the time.

Everything had changed now. He had two lives to protect and clearly he could not do it alone.

Slade opened his phone and made the call.

MAGGIE FORCED HERSELF TO nibble on some crackers and to down a bottle of water. She had checked on Slade once. He'd been standing in the small courtyard, staring at the ground. He'd made a call. She'd heard his deep voice, but he'd kept the conversation too low for her to determine who he had called or what he had called about. She had finally stopped trembling inside, but she still felt numb.

She kept thinking of her sisters and their children and whether or not her child would ever play with his cousins.

Strange that she would worry about that now. Survival should be her primary concern. Maybe that was the way her extreme anxiety manifested itself. Or maybe the idea of the children playing was survival.

A couple of days ago her biggest worry had been whether or not to continue this one-sided relationship with Slade. A smile trembled across her lips. Now she wondered if she would still be alive this time tomorrow.

The back door opened and Slade stepped inside. Her heart fluttered. She wished her body didn't respond that way whenever she laid eyes on him, but the wish was wasted. She loved looking at him…touching him… listening to his voice.

He crossed the room and sat down on the sofa directly facing her. A painful combination of fear and anticipation thumped in her chest. Was there more bad news? She, for one, wasn't sure how much more bad news she could stomach.

"There are things I need to say."

Her attention sharpened instantly. He wanted to talk? As hard as she tried not to allow the tremor to reach her hands, they shook before she could clasp them together. He noticed. And he flinched. The news must be very bad.

"My existence has been vastly different from that of most men."

She got it, fully recognized that the proclamation was the understatement of the century. There was more he wanted to say, she sensed. He braced his forearms on his knees. Maggie could have sworn she saw a bit of a tremor in his hands, as well.

"Emotional attachments were forbidden." His gray eyes connected with hers and held. "I have never felt an attachment to any person, thing or place." He looked away. "There is a connection of sorts with Alayna."

"Alayna?" Maggie tried to clear the emotion from her throat. Was this a former lover? An ache threaded through her. She had no right to feel jealous of a woman she didn't even know. Still, she did.

"She's my biological sister." He shrugged. "Half sister. There were four of us." His voice became distant as he spoke, as if he was remembering a painful time. "Two other males, myself and Alayna."

"Were?" She braced for the worst.

"The older two were terminated. One for failure to live up to the expectations of the Code, the other for betrayal."

Dear God. "She had them murdered?"

He nodded.

"What is this Code?" He had mentioned it before.

There was a long hesitation before he answered, "That's the name of the program the Dragon initiated thirty-five years ago. Her theory was related to some ancient Mayan myth about the selection and training of warriors. The belief that one molds his offspring from birth to be the perfect warrior with no other distractions like emotions. I've studied Mayan history and I could never find anything like the twisted concept she devised. She has no belief system other than in herself."

He stared at his hands as if the lines there held some clue to why he had been born to such a monster. "Four children would be born of qualifying DNA. The unknowing sperm providers would be among the most talented in the business of infiltration, intelligence gathering and assassination. The Dragon was the willing surrogate for the first four. The hope was that with the proper genetic coding inherited from our biological parents and with the intense training from the time we could walk, we would become the perfect spies. The perfect killing machines. Relentless warriors."

That was insane. The fodder of science-fiction novels. She ached to reach out to him, but she didn't dare do anything to stop the momentum.

"Two years after their termination, when I was eighteen, I escaped while on a mission. I was disillusioned by her view of our purpose." He shrugged. "I wanted a different purpose."

He'd wanted a real life. "You were instinctively repulsed by the evil she represented."

"Maybe." A frown furrowed between his eyes. "I just wanted away from her. From the place. Eventually I grew bitter and weary of hovering beneath her radar. I decided that the person responsible for my hostile childhood was my father."

"He deserted you?" Maggie had wondered if he had died or if Slade's evil mother had had him killed, as well. Slade had no one to protect him from this madwoman.

"Maybe. But I wanted to find him and I wanted him to suffer as I had." The long-festering fury in his eyes burned like molten silver.

"You found him?"

Slade nodded, again looking away. "I watched him. Drew closer at every opportunity. I couldn't wait to wield the first blow against him. To somehow make him pay for not stopping her."

Watched? Drew closer? Realization dawned with such intensity that Maggie had to remind herself to breathe. Was he talking about…?

"Rather than despising him," Slade went on, "finding fault in his every deed, I began to admire him." He rubbed his forehead. "I hated myself for the weakness. But I couldn't stop looking or yearning to be closer. He represented all that I thought I deserved and wanted… to be and could never hope to be. He had everything that is real and tangible…and I had nothing."

Maggie couldn't restrain the need any longer. She dropped to her knees, between his spread legs. She caressed his rigid jaw, savored the feel of the stubble there. "You don't give yourself credit for half the man you are. The fact that you have come this far is a testament to who you are deep inside."

He searched her eyes, his dull and listless. "How can you care so deeply for a man who is better at killing than at living?" He placed his palm between her breasts, over her heart. "What makes your heart reach out to me when my own does nothing but supply my body with oxygen?"

She tried not to show how deeply his words hurt. She had known he didn't love her the way she loved him. Not a day passed that she didn't hope, but she had known. Producing a shaky smile, she placed her hand against the center of his chest. "It works better than you think. You could have allowed that old man to die and saved yourself, but you didn't. There's more going on there than just pumping, in my opinion."

He shook his head. "That was a mistake. A split-second decision based on a misfiring neuron. The better decision would have been to ignore him and have the enemy walk away blind."

Maggie laughed. "You should stop thinking that way." She touched the bandanna around his arm. "You bleed just like I do. You have compassion and all those other emotions that you were taught to ignore. Maybe you just don't recognize them for what they are and can't utilize them to the fullest extent possible, but they're all there."

He took her face in his hands. "How can you be so sure of what I am?"

That lost little boy who only wanted someone to love him still lived inside this big, strong man. How did she help him see that he was good and caring? That his need to get away from his mother had proved that?

Maggie shared the only certainty she could prove. "I feel it every time you touch me." She blinked back the tears that threatened to make a fool of her. "You may not recognize your emotions for what they are." She was the one shrugging this time. Her own emotions were making it difficult to put her feelings into words.

She inhaled a deep breath and plunged onward. "I can't claim to know that you love me, but—" she showed him with her eyes just how genuinely she meant this "—I know you're attached to me just a little." She held her forefinger and thumb close together and attempted a smile. "Otherwise you would have left me in Chicago to fend for myself." That was the absolute truth. She felt that attachment all the way to her bones.

He leaned forward and kissed her softly, thoroughly. Maggie couldn't resist the taste, the scent of him. She leaned into the kiss.

His fingers entwined with hers and he pulled her to her feet. As if they were back home in her tiny apartment, he lifted her into his arms and carried her to the bedroom. Taking their time, as if they had all day, they undressed each other. Maggie was careful of his injured arm. He was taken with her belly, as if touching that part of her would somehow let him feel the baby growing inside her. The way he marveled at touching that part of her was all the proof she needed to know the man he was behind the abuse he had suffered.

His naked skin felt like heaven against hers. No matter what else happened, she loved being with him this way. He kissed her all over, worshipped her body with his lips and his tongue.

She'd already come twice before her pleas for him to fill her were heeded. He made love to her with that same unexpected slowness, an extra tenderness in every move. Maggie couldn't restrain her tears. They fell even as she climaxed for the third time, right along with him.

If she had needed any other proof that Slade cared deeply for her, this had been it.

And now it was too late. The Dragon would never let him go.

FOR A LONG TIME THEY LAY IN each other's arms. Slade had questions for her. He traced a path down her rib cage with his fingers. Her belly looked as smooth and flat as it had before. But it was different now. Their child was growing inside her.

"I took a pregnancy test day before yesterday," she said, evidently sensing his thoughts. "Then I took another and another." She let go a big breath. "I didn't want to believe it. I was terrified."

"How do you feel now?" Based on what she now knew about him, he couldn't imagine she was entirely happy about this turn of events.

She covered her mouth with the fingers of one hand. Her fingers shook and she blinked repeatedly. Those jewel-colored eyes shone with emotion. "I always wanted children." She managed a smile. "My sisters have kids and I love them to death." Her tongue swept over her lips to moisten them. "But having a kid involves two people and I wasn't sure how to handle that part. You didn't seem committed anywhere near that level and I'd never heard you speak of children."

Procreating was the last thing he'd envisioned himself doing, ever. He wasn't father material. Hell, he wasn't even people material.

"After my childhood," he confessed, "I hadn't planned on that route." He wouldn't lie to her about that despite the pain the words evoked in her eyes. "But I can't say that it feels wrong." He caressed her belly. The idea of her growing round with his child intrigued him, filled him with a sense of something like pride and anticipation. He wanted to be a part of this miracle.

But there was very little likelihood of that.

"That's good to hear." Disappointment shimmered in her words.

"Marek," he said, making the decision just now. "My

birth name was Tripp Marek. But I walked away from that name twelve years ago."

Happiness then gratitude glittered in her eyes. Sharing that small part of himself gave her such pleasure. "So we're sticking with Slade Keaton?"

He laughed, though the reaction had nothing to do with amusement. That was yet to be seen. After today he might not need a name. "I've gotten used to it," he admitted. "If that's what you want."

"'Used to' something is just another way of saying *attached*," she pointed out.

This time his laugh was genuine. She had a way of seeing the bright side of things. "I can't disprove your theory." He traced the soft line of her cheek. Touching her was something he didn't seem to be able to get enough of. He had certainly gotten *used to* her. All these years he had drifted through time with no roots, no attachments. He'd found Maggie and now there was no time.

"What're you going to do?" The worry she felt was evidenced in every part of her, in every word she spoke. She cared what happened to him.

How could another human care so deeply for *him*?

"I have no choice but to finish this." He had even more reason now. If the Dragon learned of Alayna's betrayal, she would be in imminent danger. If she learned of the child Maggie carried, she would revel in destroying what was his.

"Slade, I—"

He pressed his fingers to her lips. "You'll be safe. I've spoken to Jim Colby. They're in Mexico now."

"They're here?" She raised up onto her elbows. "How?"

"They've been looking for us. They're coming here to pick you up and take you back to Chicago. You'll be protected until this is over."

"Aren't they going to help you?" Worry cluttered her face.

This part he couldn't fully explain. "I can take care of myself. I want the Colby Agency's attention focused solely on keeping you safe." He flattened his palm on her belly. "This child is counting on us both."

She laced her fingers with his. "Will you be back?"

There was a question he couldn't answer. It was a fifty-fifty shot. "That's the plan."

"I don't want to put you on the spot about the baby." Determination flashed in her eyes. "If you want to come back because you want this relationship, that's great, but don't feel obligated."

Obligation hadn't entered the scenario. He couldn't describe what he felt. Not yet. This was all too new to him. But he recognized what Maggie felt. Fear. Uncertainty. Heartache. He deeply regretted that she suffered those feelings because of him.

She fidgeted with the sheet. More questions were coming. He could guess her concerns. "I'm type A positive. No known diseases or allergies. No malformations. No surgeries."

She made a face. "I hadn't even thought of that."

"But you have a question?" Or two or three. He smiled. Her desire to know him warmed him. Something else he had gotten used to.

She searched his eyes, more of that worry in hers. "Why won't you let the Colby Agency help you? How can you hope to win against her army?"

This was maybe the third time in twenty-four hours

that they had had this conversation. "No one can help." The Colby Agency would want to involve the authorities and that would be a monumental mistake. This situation would not be resolved through routine methods, particularly not legal avenues. The Dragon owned too many high-ranking members in positions of authority.

"Is it because Lucas is your father?"

He wasn't surprised that she had put two and two together. "He has no direct correlation to my decision." Was that the truth? Taking down the Dragon would surely be viewed as a triumph among men like Lucas.

"I won't keep nagging you about it," Maggie relented, "but please consider allowing them to help. If not for yourself—" she placed his hand on her belly "—for this child. This child deserves whatever you have to give him or her. Don't cheat this baby out of that opportunity."

He hushed her with a kiss. It was the only way to avoid responding to her challenge.

A child.

He was going to be a father.

If he survived the coming battle.

"Wait." A new kind of horror had claimed her expression.

Tension triggered his adrenaline. Was she in pain? "What's wrong?" His first thought was the baby.

Maggie searched his face, his eyes. "You said she was the willing surrogate of the first four... Have there been others?"

That was the other side of his nightmare. "Six. Ranging in age from eight to fourteen." He had not forgotten those children... He would not forget.

"Can we help them?"

He stroked her cheek. How had he zeroed in on the one woman who possessed the power to make him feel that compassion she wielded like a weapon? "I will stop her. And this time the Code will be broken for good."

Chapter Sixteen

2:35 p.m.

The village was too quiet. Lucas had a bad feeling deep in his gut.

Jim had parked the rented car behind an old church just off the center of town. They had walked from there. The lack of activity wouldn't have concerned Lucas since it was siesta time, but the circumstances had him on the highest level of alert.

"I've spotted three vehicles that appear out of place." Jim leaned one shoulder against the wall of a butcher shop. Lucas didn't have to be able to see his eyes beneath his dark sunglasses to know he was closely surveying the situation.

"They're here," Lucas agreed. "I can feel them." He'd been in this business too long to ignore his instincts. They were walking into an ambush. He leaned against the same wall. The question was, what were they going to do about it?

"Ian is arranging backup."

"Thomas Casey is, too," Lucas commented. "But they won't be here in time." He and Jim had driven straight here from the airfield. Jim had gotten the call from Keaton en route to meet the agency jet. Another car had been arranged for Ian and Victoria. Ian had strict orders not to let Victoria out of his sight. Lucas wanted her fully protected.

"What're your thoughts on how we should proceed? If Keaton is correct, the Dragon will make another attempt to gain access to Maggie so she can use her for bait. They may have struck already."

Lucas removed his sunglasses and tucked them into his pocket. "They're still here. They're waiting for something, but we can't wait." Lucas suspected that he was what they were waiting for. The Dragon had learned of his arrival. "Backup is too far away. We're outnumbered. We can't let this turn into a massacre."

"That would make this an even bigger tragedy."

Lucas couldn't agree more. "I'll take the car and go to Maggie. You wait for backup and give chase."

Jim straightened and crossed his arms over his chest. "You're assuming they take you both alive."

"I'm assuming that's what they're waiting for." Lucas surveyed the deserted streets. "She'll want us alive." There was no doubt. She had been toying with Lucas already. Jennifer Ashton, an old friend and trusted resource, had killed herself because of this demented woman. She'd been watching him and Victoria in Puerto Vallarta a few weeks ago. Whatever she wanted, whatever Keaton's original motives for coming to Chicago, Lucas intended to see that neither of them hurt Victoria.

The possibility that Keaton was his son and that he had been left to that twisted woman's devices had fractured Lucas's soul. Victoria had been right when she said that Keaton had likely been used and abused in every imaginable manner. How could a son have been kept from him all these years? Worse, how could he have allowed his own flesh and blood to suffer such a fate? There was no way he could have known, and still the regret ripped him apart.

Jim had been taken from Victoria and James, her first husband. But they had searched for him for years. Lucas hadn't even known to look.

But ignorance was no excuse. There was no excuse.

He had to make this right now.

"I should run this by—"

Lucas held up a hand, stopping Jim. "I don't want this to touch Victoria any more than it already has. If it's me she wants, I'm not allowing anyone else to be endangered. I don't work that way."

Jim removed his sunglasses. "I'm not certain you're thinking clearly, Lucas. The possibilities in this case are far too personal for you to make rational decisions."

There was no time to debate the issue. "I have to do this, Jim. Have you got my back?"

The pause before Jim answered rattled Lucas far more than it should have.

"Always, Lucas. Always." He slid his sunglasses back into place. "I'll be watching."

Jim walked away. Half a block down he disappeared into an alley. If any one of the Dragon's men attempted to intercept Jim, they were dead. The element of surprise in an unexpected ambush on the enemy's playing field could take a man out before he started to fight. With Jim braced for an attack in neutral territory, the attackers wouldn't have a chance.

Lucas slid his eyewear in place and walked back to the car. Maggie was waiting.

So was a war that had been a long time in coming.

MAGGIE PACED THE FLOOR. Slade had been gone for more than an hour. No one from the Colby Agency had arrived. As if that wasn't enough to have her nerves on edge, an SUV had driven past the house twice in the past fifteen minutes.

They were here.

Maggie didn't need a sign or a knock on the door. She could feel the evil pressing closer.

She couldn't wait any longer. A weapon and a hiding place were critical.

She stared at the handgun on the table. Slade had left that for her. Not one time in her life had she fired a weapon. He'd shown her how to take the safety off, how to take aim and how to fire.

Could she point it at a living, breathing human and do it? Maggie didn't know.

To save her life and that of her child? Yes, of course. But the hesitation Slade had warned her about would be the only mistake necessary to cost her both those precious things.

She picked up the gun. It felt even heavier than it had when he'd insisted she hold it. She inhaled a deep, solidifying breath. Now for the hiding place.

There didn't appear to be a cellar. No closets. There was just one place.

Under the bed.

The gun clutched tightly in her right hand, Maggie checked the door locks once more, then walked to the bedroom. The tangled sheets tugged at her heart. She and Slade had made love here only a few hours ago. Closing her eyes, she prayed again for his protection.

Getting on her knees, she checked under the bed.

Nothing but dust bunnies. Trying not to breathe in

the dust, she scooted under the bed. The space was cramped, so she lay flat, her face and her weapon aimed at the door. If anyone came into the room and looked under the bed, she intended to squeeze the trigger just like Slade said.

The minutes ticked off in her head, keeping time with her pounding heart. She alternately prayed and cried until she felt exhausted. Closing her eyes, she focused on thoughts of the future. Would her baby be a boy or a girl? Would she keep running the coffee shop or hire a manager so she could be a full-time mom?

The front door creaked.

Maggie's eyes flew open and her heart stumbled.

A click signaled the door had closed. Footsteps on the tile floor were so soft, she scarcely heard the sound. Maybe she only sensed the noise since she knew for sure someone had come inside.

Maggie released the safety on the weapon and adjusted her hold on the butt.

The roar of blood rushing through her brain drowned out any other noise. The intruder or intruders would be searching the house. It was only a matter of seconds before this room would come under scrutiny.

She had left the bedroom door open. Maggie saw the shoes before she heard the man's approach. He moved around the room. To the far side of the bed. To the window. She saw the hem of the curtain near the floor shift as he looked outside.

She stopped breathing as the toes of his shoes came to rest next to the bed. Moving one tiny increment at a time, she shifted her aim toward that side of the bed.

The intruder turned. One knee went down on the floor.

Maggie's hands shook.

A face appeared.

Her fingers went limp. The gun clattered to the floor.

Lucas.

She was sobbing hard by the time he helped her to her feet. He hugged her until the hysteria subsided.

"They're here," she said when she found her voice.

Lucas nodded. "I know."

"How will we escape?"

The front door burst inward. Then the rear.

Lucas pulled her behind him and leveled his weapon on the bedroom door.

Dear God. They were coming.

Chapter Seventeen

Maggie sat very still in the chair to which one of the men had tied her. Across the room, the woman who called herself the Dragon spoke quietly with the men who had brought them here.

Lucas sat a few feet away. The entire trip here, tied up in the cargo area of the SUV, he had whispered reassurances to Maggie. Despite the black bags over their heads, hearing his voice had kept her from losing her mind to the panic. Once they had arrived the bags had been removed as if their captors wanted them to see that there was no escape.

This place was like a prison. A huge compound with a towering wall protecting it from any outside threat. The interior was massive and austere. The stark spaces were frightening and cold. Several large monitors were mounted on the wall in this room. Information and images streamed on each one. The interrogation room, the woman had called it. There was nothing enduring or homey about any part of this place that Maggie had seen. The idea that Slade grew up in this heinous institution-like setting squeezed Maggie's heart painfully.

She and Lucas had not been questioned, but Maggie imagined that was coming. Soon. The band around her neck chafed her skin. It wasn't a part of the restraints. But both she and Lucas had been fitted with one when they were dragged into this room. Maggie wondered if it was a GPS device of some sort.

As if she had telegraphed her thoughts, the Dragon turned and strode across the room. Maggie shuddered inwardly. The woman looked so much like Victoria. It was uncanny. Disturbing.

"Where is he?"

Since she stared at Maggie, she assumed the evil witch was talking to her. "He left." She infused as much strength in her voice as she could muster. "He's never coming back. You won't find him." Pride welled inside her at how she'd managed to get it all out. "He didn't tell me where he was going," she added.

A palm collided with her jaw, sending her head snapping back. Maggie shook herself, blinked back the tears and glared at the woman who had slapped her. "You asked." Her cheek and lip throbbed. "Wasn't I supposed to answer?"

The Dragon shook her head. "You are quite pathetic. What he saw in you escapes me. I trained him better than that. I suppose there is no accounting for taste."

Maggie refused to let those ugly words touch her heart. She also held her tongue. Pushing the woman would only get her hurt and Maggie had to protect her baby. The thought of the life growing in her womb made her smile inside. That was one secret this witch would never know. She didn't deserve to know.

"Why don't you let her go," Lucas suggested. "It's me you really want."

The Dragon laughed, the sound anything but humorous. "Don't flatter yourself, Lucas. There was a time when that was indeed the case, but that time has long passed. You are of no significance to me."

Lucas laughed. "Ah, but you remain significant to me and a number of others. There are so very many out there who still want you. The CIA and Interpol have never stopped looking for you. They're getting closer than you know."

The witch smiled. "And they will keep looking." She leaned down to put her face in his. "No one can stop me. But then—" she straightened "—you knew that, didn't you? You wouldn't be here had I not ordered your presence. I gave the order and—" she smiled "—here you are."

A smirk twisted Lucas's lips. "Do you really believe your underlings brought me in against my will? I knew they were coming. I wanted to be here."

Fury whipped across the woman's face. "Really?" She turned to her men, considered each for a trauma-filled moment. "Well? What say you?"

The two who had driven Maggie and Lucas to this awful place exchanged a look. One said, "He had a weapon. We disarmed and secured him."

Lucas shook his head. "How many did I eliminate before you disarmed me?"

"None," the man said. "We were—"

"Fool," the Dragon screeched. "If he wanted one or more of you dead, you would be dead." She adjusted the elegant suit jacket she wore. "Get out."

The men obeyed, leaving the Dragon alone with Maggie and Lucas.

"I came for my son."

Maggie stared at Lucas. What was he doing? Was he purposely trying to inflame her?

More of that red-hot fury slashed across the Dragon's face. "Your son? There you go flattering yourself again. You were the sperm donor, nothing more."

Lucas shrugged one shoulder. "He considers me his father. I guess that makes it real enough. Does he call you *mother*?"

"Before I end your pathetic existence," she warned, ignoring his question, "why don't you tell me where he is and end this tedious business."

"He's gone, Dragon," Lucas said with audible pleasure. "He isn't coming back. I assured him that I would square things with you."

The Dragon glanced at Maggie. "Perhaps I'll spare his little friend if you make this easy for me."

"She doesn't know where he is, either. Anything you do to her will be a waste of time and energy. You've got me. You don't need anyone else."

Before she could toss another warning at him, he added, "Did you say *easy*?" Lucas cut loose with another of those deep, throaty laughs. "You getting soft in your old age?"

She strode up to him and reached down. As Maggie watched in horror, she grabbed Lucas by the right ankle and ripped off his prosthetic leg. She tossed it across the room. "Age is just a number, wouldn't you say?" She dusted her palms together. "It's the mind and *body* that make the man. There isn't a stronger, more powerful man alive than this woman."

In a move so fast and so fluid, Lucas drew his left knee to his chest and kicked her in the stomach. She hit the floor flat on her back. Lucas propelled himself, chair and all, on top of her.

Maggie bit back a scream. What should she do?

Three men rushed into the room. Maggie cried out a warning as she watched Lucas, still secured to the chair, struggle with the evil woman.

Two of the men dragged Lucas off her. His mouth was bloody. Maggie's breath caught as she spied the gash in the Dragon's cheek.

"Prepare him," she ordered, swiping at the blood with the back of her hand. The third man hurried to her with a cloth to hold on the wound. "I will watch you die," she snarled at Lucas. "I had planned a special ceremony, but it's clear you are in a hurry."

"You have no right to wear her face," Lucas thundered. "I will cut it off you myself."

With her two goons holding Lucas down, the Dragon moved close to him once more. "You were so besotted with her it was sickening. Pathetic. Your precious Victoria was another man's wife. I knew changing my face to look like hers would get me what I needed."

"You were that desperate? You needed to transform yourself into someone else?" Lucas didn't let up with his verbal assault. "Are you quite sure I was the pathetic one?"

"You were the target," she blasted right back. "It was my mission to know everything about you. Like how you saved your best friend in a POW camp." She pointed to his missing leg. "You paid a dear price for your loyalty. How honorable of you. Or were you just hoping to impress his fiancée?" She leaned closer still.

"I knew your every secret, Lucas. Your record at the CIA was unparalleled for such a young man. You were the perfect candidate for my needs. Just ask your old friend Jennifer. She can tell you I always get what I want. But she's dead. I suppose she can't confirm that for me." She shrugged. "I let her know I planned a visit and she went and checked out before I arrived. How rude."

Maggie's stomach dropped to her feet. The horror stories Slade had told her were all true. It wasn't that she hadn't believed him...yet it was so unbelievable. "But your big plan failed."

It wasn't until the woman glowered at Maggie that she realized she had spoken the words aloud. Fear exploded in her chest as the woman moved toward her.

"What did he tell you?" she demanded.

It was too late for Maggie to take back what she'd said.

The Dragon turned to her cohort. "Give her the Sodium Pentothal. She'll talk."

The baby! Maggie couldn't let them give her drugs. "The Code. I know about the Code."

The look in the Dragon's eyes was indescribable. Rage. Hysteria. Insanity. "You're lying."

"We both know about the Code," Lucas said, drawing her attention back to him. "Did you think you could keep your secret forever?"

How did Lucas know? Was he bluffing?

The Dragon laughed. "You have no idea what I have accomplished."

"There were four," Maggie said quickly, drawing the fire from Lucas. "Three males and one female. Two failed. They couldn't live up to your warrior standards.

So you terminated them. Only Tripp and Alayna are left and their allegiance is not to you." Maggie prayed she got the details right. Her head was spinning.

"Shut her up," the Dragon roared.

One of the men moved toward Maggie. "You won't have any better luck with the new ones," she shouted before the man reached her. "They'll turn on you just like the others. Then you'll have no one to torture and abuse. You'll be alone."

He grabbed Maggie's chin. She braced for the worst. He attempted to open her mouth. She fought to keep it closed. But he was strong. Her lips and teeth parted. He stuffed a cloth into her mouth.

The Dragon glared at Maggie for a long moment before ordering, "Raise the alert. Evacuate the six." Her attention moved from Lucas to Maggie and back. "These two are foolishly bluffing, but we won't take the risk."

"Don't waste your time," Lucas said, his voice oddly weary. "Your game is over."

What was wrong with Lucas? Maggie tried to see around the goon hovering over him. When he stepped back, she saw the IV-like bag hanging on the back of Lucas's chair. A line ran to his chest and disappeared beneath his shirt. Were they giving him the drug they had talked about? Maggie had heard of it before. Truth serum.

The Dragon leaned down to look Lucas in the eyes. "This drug takes a full two hours to destroy the human body from the inside out. It's a slower method than I had initially intended, but so far it has gotten rave reviews from others." She smiled. "It's new and I've been dying to try it out." She flashed that smile at Maggie. "Say goodbye to your pathetic little friend."

Desperation erupted inside Maggie.

"Get Raby in here," the Dragon ordered.

Maggie watched the man rush out of the room. What now? The need to heave ached in her throat. She closed her eyes and prayed hard that someone would come to rescue them. That this evil woman would not have her way again.

The witch laughed long and loud. Maggie's eyes flew open. A new man had arrived, this one older and unarmed. He ushered the Dragon into a chair and seemed to be tending to the wound on her cheek.

"Are you praying?" the Dragon asked Lucas. She shook her head. "Pathetic."

Maggie's throat and eyes burned. She turned to Lucas. His head had lolled to one side. Her chest constricted with panic. She was killing him. Maggie had to do something.

"Can you take care of this, Raby?"

Maggie's attention swung back to the Dragon and the man working on her face.

"Of course. Once it's healed, I'll make it go away. At the moment we just need to get it closed to avoid infection. Now, be still."

Maggie's eyes widened as she watched. Raby ordered a tray. When the stainless-steel tray loaded with instruments arrived, he began stitching the wound. Maggie replayed those last few steps. The man had not injected any sort of anesthetic. The Dragon never even flinched as the needle slid through her skin.

Maggie blinked, felt herself sinking into the escape

offered by her mind's denial. She fought the lure. *Have to stay alert...to pay attention.*

The Dragon stared at her. She smirked. "After enough Botox you lose all sensation."

When Raby had applied a small bandage to the sutured wound, the Dragon pushed him away. He hurried from the room without once glancing at the hostages. Maggie didn't blame him. See no evil, fear no evil.

The Dragon stalked over to Lucas and lifted his head. "Feels good, doesn't it?" She laughed. "I understand the intense burning is the worst. It's the buildup of the toxin that actually kills you. That's why it can't be a single injection. Why don't you weigh in for us, Mr. Master Spy?" She sighed. "You really threw a wrinkle into my plans. I wanted you to watch your son die before we reached this point, but I guess we'll just go with plan B."

Think, Maggie! Do something!

She started moaning. Talking was not happening with the gag stuck in her mouth. The goon standing near her yanked her by the hair. She screamed as best she could around the gag. The Dragon turned to her. Maggie nodded and groaned as loud as she could. She widened her eyes in hopes of making the woman understand she had something she needed to say.

"What is she trying to say?" The Dragon dropped Lucas's head and strode toward Maggie.

The gag was yanked from Maggie's mouth. She gasped, bit back the instinct to retch.

"You have something to say?" The Dragon grabbed a handful of Maggie's hair and jerked her head back. "I hate when my time is wasted."

"Lucas didn't tell you the whole truth." Maggie's

head felt as if it was going to explode. She wasn't in the spy business. She didn't know how to do this. But she had to do something. Making stuff up was the only option she could think of.

The Dragon's gaze narrowed. "I'm waiting."

"A…a CIA team is on the way. He made it easy for your men to catch him because that team was going to follow us here." Maggie had no idea if that made sense. She didn't have a clue if the CIA had teams. Dear God, please let her desperate plan buy them some time.

The Dragon turned to one of her henchmen. "Stop the IV. We may need him."

Relief rushed through Maggie. Thank God.

The Dragon approached her. "If you're lying, I will make your final hours more painful than you can possibly imagine."

"It's the truth," Maggie urged. "I heard him talking to whoever is in charge."

"Thomas Casey," Lucas said, his voice weak.

Maggie's chest inflated with new hope. He was still alive and, evidently, she had done well. He was running with the story she had started.

"Casey?" The Dragon strolled across the room and studied one of the monitors mounted on the wall. "He is on the move." She turned back to Lucas. "I keep tabs on certain high-level members of competition."

"I'll let him know you consider him competition." Lucas licked his lips. His words were sluggish as he continued, "FYI, he considers you a crazy bitch."

Outrage practically radiated off the Dragon. She started toward Lucas, murder in her eyes.

"Dragon."

She wheeled to face the man who had spoken. "What?"

He appeared to be listening to a voice in his earpiece. His expression reflected the emotions generated by the news.

"There's been a security breach," he finally announced. "Sector three."

The Dragon's attention swung back to Lucas. Maggie was afraid to breathe.

"How many are there?" she demanded of Lucas.

Lucas stared at her but said nothing.

Terror ignited in Maggie's heart.

"How many?" the Dragon screamed.

"Only one."

Maggie gasped. She twisted to see the man who had spoken.

Slade.

As he stepped into the room, Maggie's heart sang. He was alive.

He kicked the door shut, then reached behind him and set the lock, never allowing his full attention to deviate from the woman who had given birth to him. Maggie frowned. Part of her was so thankful to see him. But this woman intended to kill him. He shouldn't be here.

"You!" the Dragon snarled.

One corner of Slade's mouth lifted in a half smile. "Hello, Mother."

Chapter Eighteen

"I wouldn't do that if I were you," Slade warned as Eli Kennemore, the Dragon's chief of security, reached for his weapon. He pointed to his bulky vest, then showed off a small gadget he wore like a watch. "Unless you want to see just how high *sky high* is."

Kennemore's hand dropped away from his shoulder holster. A blur of movement snagged Slade's attention as another of the guards drew his weapon. Slade put a bullet between his eyes before he had the barrel leveled on his target.

"How about you?" he said to the remaining guard. "The button?" He held up his left hand. "Or a bullet?"

The guy's hands went up in surrender.

"Now that we're all here," the Dragon announced, drawing the attention of the room to her, "why don't we get this little family reunion under way."

"Untie her," Slade ordered. He had no interest in intellectual discourse. "Now!" he added when no one in the room reacted.

"Did you really believe it would be this simple?" the Dragon asked. "You breach the perimeter, take out a guard or two and then barge in here to play the hero?"

She shook her head. "You greatly overestimated your-self. Let's show your girlfriend how quickly you fall."

A streak of uncertainty licked at Slade's determina-tion. "You," he said to the guard with his hands still in the air, "untie her."

"Look at the band she's wearing," the Dragon sug-gested. "Do you recognize it?"

Fear slammed into Slade. Both Maggie and Lucas wore a silver band around their necks. One click of the remote and the band would tighten into itself until it was no larger than a bracelet.

"Take it off her." He had never wanted to kill anyone the way he wanted to kill this heartless murderer. "Take it off!"

The Dragon shook her head. "Remove the explosives and lower your weapon."

Despite the fear pounding in his temples, Slade held his ground. Any sign of weakness and the Dragon would devour him. "Let them go and I'll do exactly that." Surviving wasn't his top priority. But Maggie's survival was. And Lucas's. Slade didn't want him to die for reasons he couldn't begin to decipher just now. And he needed to find Alayna.

"You'll do it anyway." The Dragon walked up to him, completely fearless. "Or they will die."

He wanted to kill her so badly his entire soul howled with the need. "Let them go and you'll still have time to eliminate me before you have to evacuate."

The look in her eyes suggested she believed him. The concern that flickered startled him. "Who's heading the team?" she demanded. "Thomas Casey?"

Slade didn't know what the hell she was talking about, but if it worked to his advantage he would go with it. "I don't know who's in charge, but I do know their goal. Destroy you and this compound. No one wants to admit you've been operating under their radar all this time, so they're going to pretend you never existed."

"Put down your weapons. Give me the detonator and I'll let them live."

Slade knew that strategy. He'd used it many times. He could live with that. "Remove the bands first."

The seconds of silence that followed had him sweating.

"Remove hers," the Dragon ordered. "Leave his." When Kennemore had done as she asked, Slade placed his weapon on the floor. Taking his time, he removed the vest and the detonator, placed them on the floor, as well. She would kill him, but not until she was certain he posed no other threat. Right now he had her worried. He turned his hands palms up. "We don't have a lot of time. They're out there."

"Take them outside," she said to her chief of security. "Then see that the evac is nearing completion."

Whatever had spooked her, she had activated the evacuation strategy. Did that mean Alayna was gone? She was among the first to go in the plan. Slade had planned to prompt the Dragon to initiate that very strategy. Someone had done him a favor.

He couldn't meet Maggie's eyes as she was untied and taken from the room. Lucas leaned heavily on the two guards. Slade could imagine what the Dragon had done to him, judging by the bag hanging on his chair. The guard grabbed his prosthetic leg on the way out.

When the room was cleared, his mother stared at him for a very long time. "You were everything I had hoped you would be. But you betrayed me."

The hatred ran so thick and hot in his veins that it literally burned. "You betrayed *me* at birth."

"I guess we're even then." She laughed. "Too bad, I set the rules and you know what they are. Shall we get to the point? I have a flight to catch."

He needed to wait for just the right moment. Yet he needed to hurry. The guards would no more set Maggie and Lucas free than the dead guy over there would. The one advantage he had was the Dragon was in a hurry to get out of here. She would not take chances with her own survival.

He held his arms wide apart. "I guess I'm as ready as I'll ever be."

She was suspicious. He read it in her body language. But she was also in a hurry. "You weren't like the others." The tiniest hint of regret colored her tone. "You were a masterpiece. Brilliant in every way."

That she lingered surprised him. There was just one answer he would like to have before he finished this. He might as well ask. "Was there ever a moment that you genuinely loved any of us? Felt guilt for what you'd done?"

She moved her head side to side, disdain in her eyes. "You've lost your edge. You wouldn't last long out there like this."

Maybe, maybe not. But she wasn't going to last the next few minutes.

"We should move on to the termination room." She gestured to the door as if she had just invited him to dinner. "I'll allow you to view their exodus prior to termination." She smiled. "You see, I'm not a complete monster."

He knew she was lying, but that was irrelevant. If he timed his move just right, his plan could work.

Slade led the way out of the room. With the evac in progress no one would be around to stop him. He would have the Dragon all to himself.

THE SUN SAT LOW ON THE mountains behind the compound as they crossed the yard toward the main gate. The stone wall looked even more menacing the second time Maggie laid eyes on it. She wanted to run back to the massive entry door and scream Slade's name.

Were these guards really going to let them go? She rubbed at her neck where the band had been. Lucas still wore his. He was leaning on one of the guards. Maggie prayed he hadn't gotten enough of that toxin in his system to do permanent damage. He didn't look good.

She looked around, vaguely wondered where the other guards were. Had the evacuation been that thorough? When she looked back at the building they had exited, she got a nudge in the lower back for her trouble.

Did Slade have an alternate plan? He'd given up his weapons. How was he supposed to fight the Dragon unarmed?

Her stomach lurched at the thought that he could be in serious trouble right now. There was no one to help him. Why hadn't he allowed the Colby Agency to help? Why had Lucas come to her alone?

This was all wrong.

Tears welled in her eyes. Dammit. She did not want Slade to die.

Lucas dropped to his knees. Maggie turned to see if

he was all right, but her guard grabbed her by the hair and pulled her back.

"Get up," the one who seemed to be in charge demanded of Lucas.

Lucas didn't respond. His head lolled forward. Was he dying? "He needs help," Maggie cried. "Can't you see that?" When the guard did nothing, she shouted, "Help him!"

As the guard hovered over the older man, Lucas moved like lightning. He rammed his elbow into the guy's groin. The guard buckled forward. Lucas grabbed his weapon and shot to his feet. He leveled it on the man holding her. "Let her go."

The guard shoved the muzzle of his gun against her head. "Drop the weapon," he warned. "Don't think I won't kill her. Our orders are to kill you both at the gate."

The explosion that shattered the silence deafened Maggie. The guard clutching her jerked back. Something warm and wet splattered her cheek. His hold on her released and he crumpled to the ground, an angry hole in the center of his forehead.

"That's what I figured." Lucas lowered his weapon.

Maggie couldn't move. Couldn't speak.

The guard on his knees suddenly pointed something at Lucas. "Watch out!" The words pealed out of Maggie's throat.

Lucas spun around and fired another shot. The man slumped over.

Maggie turned all the way around. The whole place seemed empty. The silence was almost as deafening as the gunshots.

A weapon hit the ground near her feet. Her sluggish reactions forced her attention upward. Lucas was clutching at the silver band around his neck. His eyes bulged and he was gasping for breath.

Maggie reached for the band. It tightened around her fingers even as she tried to pry between it and Lucas's throat. It was choking him. He tried to say something, but couldn't get the words out. He pointed to the guard slumped over on the ground.

There had to be a key or something. She pushed the man over. Ignoring the hole where his nose used to be, she searched his pockets.

Lucas dropped to his knees. Maggie's movements turned frantic. There was no key! Nothing but a cell phone and a pack of cigarettes. "There isn't a key!" Lucas's face was beet red.

Something small and dark on the sandy ground captured her attention. A gadget about the size of a cigarette lighter. She grabbed it and, smoothing her thumb over the surface, felt something like a button. She pressed it, knowing this was her last and only hope.

Lucas gasped.

She turned to him just in time to see the silver band pop loose and drop to the ground. She hurried over to him, trudging through the sand on her knees.

"You okay, Lucas?" His weight fell against her. She lowered him to the ground and once again panic started to build inside her. She needed help!

His mouth and eyes were open. His face wasn't so red anymore, but he wouldn't respond to her. She leaned down, put her cheek close to his nose and mouth. He wasn't breathing. She checked his pulse. Nothing. Oh, dear God!

Instinct kicked in. Maggie assumed the CPR position, tilted his head back as she pinched his nose closed and blew air into his mouth. She mentally counted off the puffs, then did the required number of chest compressions. Again. She repeated the series. *Please don't die!*

After a few more rounds of compressions and breaths, she thought she heard a shallow gasp. She checked Lucas's pulse again. There it was. Relief spewed through her limbs.

His eyes opened and she almost fainted. "You scared me to death."

He tried to smile, but a cough stopped him.

"Can you get up?" She wanted to get back in there and check on Slade.

Lucas elbowed his way to a sitting position. "I think I can manage."

The crack of gunshots shattered the silence.

Lucas pulled Maggie to the ground and covered her body with his own.

Who was shooting at them? They had no cover. The weapons were too far away to reach.

Maggie raised her head far enough to stare back at the house. Somehow she had to get back in there.

As if to dissuade her, a bullet hit the sand next to her head.

THE CORRIDORS WERE DESERTED. Each room Slade passed was the same. In the sprawling kitchen was a door that led to a basement level. That was where all on-site terminations were carried out.

"Has Alayna left already?" he asked as they descended the stairs.

"You cost your sister more than you know by dragging her into your betrayal."

She knew.

Slade's insides turned to ice.

"Where is she?" He turned on the Dragon. "Where is Alayna?"

The Dragon gestured across the room. "I wanted to be able to admire her beauty, so I arranged a special place for her."

The bottom dropped out of Slade's stomach as he rushed to the containment vessel that encapsulated Alayna. She stared back at him with unseeing eyes. Her slim body was naked and the bright blue-green dragon tattoo that marked her stood out against her pale skin.

Renewed rage detonated inside him.

He turned to face the monster who had done this. Whatever had cut her face, he wished it had torn her whole head off.

"You killed her, just like the others."

She shook her head. "You killed her. Now it's your turn. Only, you'll be incinerated like the others. Not a single trace will be left."

She slapped at him, but he dodged her hand. The ring she always wore was turned downward so that the massive faux stone served as a weapon. A lethal weapon. The Dragon always wore that poison ring. It was her trademark maneuver when taking out an enemy up close.

Slade grabbed her wrist, kept her hand and the ring away from his throat. The carotid artery was her preferred target. This time there was no one here to back up the Dragon and he was physically far stronger than her. It was psychological power she had always held over him. She struggled ferociously.

No more. It was over.

"You wouldn't dare kill me!" the Dragon roared. "I created you!"

From the corner of his eye, Alayna snagged his attention. She stared unseeing at him through the glass. Sweet Alayna. She had done nothing to deserve this awful end.

Slade ruthlessly twisted the Dragon's hand around and slammed her palm into her own throat. Her eyes rounded in surprise.

He pressed harder, forcing the toxin into her body. Then he released her.

She staggered back, her arms falling to her sides.

He watched without blinking. He wanted to relish every moment of this.

Then he wanted her to burn as she had planned for him.

The Dragon's eyes closed for the last time.

Slade checked her pulse and then loaded her body into the incinerator. He hit the switch as he turned away. The sound of the flames igniting was music to his ears.

Right now he had to find Maggie. And Lucas.

Kennemore was the Dragon's closest confidant and ally. Slade didn't trust him one little bit with Maggie and Lucas.

Slade said one last goodbye to Alayna, then he raced up to the ground level without encountering another living being. He snagged a weapon from one of the downed security men. Those who hadn't been terminated were likely already in the evac tunnel.

He paused at the front entrance of the place he had

once called home and listened. No sound of exchanging gunfire, but he could hear voices.

Weapon readied for firing, Slade leaned far enough into the opening to visually assess the situation.

Maggie was hugging someone. Lucas was on the ground with Jim Colby and Victoria hovering over him.

Slade stepped out into the dusk and headed that way.

He knew the moment Maggie saw him. She stood up and rushed to him, throwing her arms around his neck. "I was so afraid for you."

He let her hug him for as long as she needed to. When she drew back, she had twenty questions. Was he okay? Was the danger over now? Had he slain the Dragon?

Jim Colby approached them. When Maggie looked up, he said, "We have a MedFlight copter en route to transport Lucas to a trauma center."

"Will he be all right?" Maggie pressed.

"I believe so," Jim assured her. "He's a tough guy."

"Thank God." Maggie sagged against Slade about the same instant Jim's attention swung to him.

"You're unharmed?"

Slade nodded. "She initiated the evac plan," he went on to explain. "The others…the files for the Code—all of it is escaping through the mountains, as we speak."

"The CIA and Interpol are already on it," Jim explained. "They have the group secured."

Slade felt a sense of relief like he had never before experienced.

It was over.

His attention settled on Lucas. Victoria hovered over him, caressing him and whispering to him. Slade couldn't help wondering what it felt like to love someone that much.

What it felt like to love someone at all.

Maggie smiled up at him. She deserved someone to love her the way Victoria loved Lucas.

Slade wished he could be that man. For Maggie and for the baby.

But he wasn't.

Chapter Nineteen

Colby Agency, Chicago,
October 28, 4:05 p.m.

Victoria was the last to settle at the conference-room table. The others waited silently, the tension thick enough to taste. She immediately reached for Lucas's hand. A week in the hospital had cleared the toxin from his system. He remained a little weak, but he was gaining strength every day. For that she was eternally grateful.

She surveyed the faces around her. Jim, Simon, Ian and Slade Keaton. This meeting had been called to clear the air once and for all. She also had a surprise announcement regarding the agreement she and Lucas had reached while he was hospitalized. But that would come later.

"I'm glad we've all finally found the time to meet." The past twelve days had been a whirlwind of activities and changes.

Slade met her gaze and she smiled. This had been the hardest on him. Days of intense interrogation by both the CIA and Interpol had cleared him of any possible charges based on the extenuating circumstances that surrounded his childhood. He had gone back to Mexico and ensured a proper burial for his sister. Then he had helped the CIA dismantle the Dragon's fortress of horrors. Jim had stepped forward and volunteered to assist him with both efforts. Victoria hoped a bond would form between the two men; after all, they were brothers in a way.

Ian was first on the meeting's agenda. "Keaton, we've deliberated at length and we've reached an agreement."

Slade looked from Ian to Victoria and back. He was one of the strongest men Victoria had met and still his trepidation was immense. Only because she had come to know him so well could she see that uncertainty. This told Victoria far more than anything else about the man. He cared. Few who had survived what he had, with no nurturing foundation whatsoever, could grow as much. Her son, Jim, had at least had the first seven years of his life to achieve that foundation before being ripped from his real home by a monster not unlike the Dragon.

"Before you say more," Slade spoke up, "I realize that most, if not all, of you have no reason to trust me."

Jim held up a hand. "Take it from me, Keaton. What you did is not the worst anyone at this table has done. If the majority of us weren't prepared to trust you, you wouldn't be here today."

Leave it to Jim to cut straight to the chase. Her son was very much like his father. Victoria was incredibly proud of him.

Slade scrubbed a hand over his chin. "I appreciate your vote of confidence. But I still owe all of you an apology." He laughed and directed the next comment to Jim. "Take it from me, that doesn't happen often."

There were a few chuckles and the tension eased a fraction.

"I have a long way to go," Slade confessed, "but I have every intention of ensuring that the rest of my life matters." He glanced at Lucas. "I finally found the path I want to take and an excellent role model to help me stay on the right track."

Pride welled in Victoria. Lucas and Slade had worked out the details of their relationship. The mutual respect had been apparent. The ground was still a little shaky, but the two had an excellent start.

"With that in mind," Ian continued, "the Colby Agency would like to offer you a position here. Jim and I would also like to extend that same offer to any of your team from the Equalizers, since you don't plan to reopen."

The surprise on Slade's face warmed Victoria's heart. From the moment she had learned that Slade was Lucas's son, she had hoped this moment would come.

Slade laughed. "It would be far more polite for me to say that this is a huge surprise." He shook his head. "But the fact is, I have watched you for nearly two years. Each time you banded together to help those who darken your door or even in support of each other, I was certain the act was just for show. The occasional good deed. No one was that giving and that caring all the time."

Expectant silence reigned in the room.

"But I was wrong. You are not only the best at what you do, you care." He shook his head again. "I'm not sure I measure up to those standards."

Victoria started to disagree but Slade held up a hand.

He looked from one face to the other, lastly settling his gaze on Lucas. "That said, if you're willing to give me this opportunity on a probationary basis, you have my word that I will do everything within my power to meet those standards."

Jim clapped him on the back. "The position is yours, Keaton."

A round of applause filled the room.

The door opened and Mildred Ballard, Victoria's longtime assistant, led the rest of the gang into the room. Nichole, Ian's wife, Jolie, Simon's wife, and Tasha, Jim's wife, followed, their arms loaded with champagne and glasses.

Corks popped. Stemmed champagne flutes were filled and passed around the room.

Lucas held his flute high for all to see. "A toast." The crowd quieted instantly. He turned to Slade. "To the newest member of the family. Please welcome Slade Keaton, my son."

Emotion made Victoria's lips tremble as cheers resounded in the conference room. This was as it should be. She sipped her champagne, then caught up with her husband and kissed him on the cheek.

"I am so proud of you, Lucas." She wrapped her arm around his. "You are an amazing man."

Lucas lifted an eyebrow and eyed her skeptically. "If we're taking another vacation, let's go north this time."

Victoria laughed. "I'm not buttering you up for a vacation." She searched his face, her thoughts turning serious. "You're still sure about what we discussed?"

He nodded. "One hundred percent."

Anticipation sang through her veins. "Shall we?"

"Absolutely."

Victoria squeezed his arm before moving to the conference table to refill her flute. She tasted the sweet wine and then lifted it high to garner the room's attention once more.

When all was quiet, she began with a nervous glance at her husband. Victoria actually felt giddy. "I have two very important announcements." A rumble went around the room. Simon, Ian and Jim exchanged a look. They were aware of her first announcement, but they knew nothing of the second.

"For more than a quarter century the Colby Agency has operated solely from Chicago. Until four years ago we had used the same building for all that time." She searched the faces of the people who made up her extended family. The most honorable and compassionate men and women to be found anywhere. She loved them all. "Our clients come to us from far and wide. We serve their needs with the utmost discretion. We *are* the very best."

More applause and cheers reverberated in the room.

"But we want to do more. With that in mind, the Colby Agency is branching out. We're opening an office in the great state of Texas next spring." Victoria waited for the applause to settle once more. "Simon will be heading the office." She sent Simon a pointed look. "He has been informed that he may not recruit from this office." Laughter roared. "He may, however, borrow help for a time to get things off the ground. Simon is scouting locations now. We should have a new Colby address soon."

Victoria waited with her second announcement while cheers and congratulations were exchanged. This was Simon's moment. He deserved the well-wishes and congratulations.

Besides, it gave Victoria a moment to fortify herself

with another glass of champagne. Watching these wonderful people inundated her with second thoughts. Were she and Lucas doing the right thing? It was the biggest decision they had made since deciding to get married.

Mildred, not only Victoria's longtime assistant but also her closest girlfriend, huddled with Victoria. She took Victoria's free hand and squeezed it. "Don't lose your nerve, Victoria," she urged. "You and Lucas deserve this."

Mildred was right. Victoria hugged her and nodded. "We do deserve this."

Mildred clinked her glass with Victoria's, then rejoined the crowd.

Lucas moved to Victoria's side. "Shall we?"

Victoria's lips slid into a smile. The timing was right. She lifted her glass once more and waited for the excitement to settle.

"I have one final announcement." She met Lucas's gaze. "Lucas and I have decided that it's time to retire."

The shocked silence that Victoria had expected fell over the room. She took a breath and forged on. "We're looking for a winter home in Texas, so we'll be frequent visitors at both offices. But we will no longer be involved with day-to-day operations." She surveyed the astonished faces. "We leave the work in trusted hands."

Jim raised his glass. "Hear! Hear!"

The cheers and congratulations erupted in the room. Tear-filled hugs were exchanged. Victoria personally assured each member of her staff that she and Lucas would always be around.

Eventually she made her way to her office for a moment alone.

Victoria trailed her fingers across her well-polished

mahogany desk—the same desk James had used. It was one of the few pieces that had survived the explosion four years ago. She smiled at the memories of how they had searched for weeks to find just the right offices and then the perfect pieces of furniture. They had made love on this desk the night after it was delivered.

Her eyes burned with the recollection of the pain that had come next. Jim's abduction, then her husband's murder. A lone tear slid down her cheek.

Victoria took a deep breath and moved to the window. She looked out at the city she loved and serenity settled over her. Though this wasn't the exact window, the view was the same. This view had helped her find comfort during those days when she wasn't certain she could survive another day. When Jim was missing, she would watch the children go by, searching each face for her son's. After her husband's death she had used the view as her private theater for replaying the precious moments she and James had shared.

Victoria turned back to the desk and considered that she and Lucas had sat across from each other at this desk for all those years as she survived the agony of crushing loss. He was there for her every step of the way. And he waited patiently as her respect and friendship grew into a deep, meaningful love.

She had been truly blessed.

"There you are."

Lucas joined her at the window. "I'm afraid we stole the show in there." He draped his arm around her. "They're all happy for us, my dear."

Victoria leaned her forehead against his cheek. "It's the beginning of a new adventure."

Lucas hugged her closer. "That I can promise."

Victoria spotted a familiar figure crossing the street below. She leaned closer to the window and studied the man. "Isn't that Slade?" Had he left the celebration early? She hoped he was as happy with his new life as they were to have him in theirs.

"It is." Lucas pointed to the coffee shop across the street. "See where he's headed."

Victoria smiled. Happiness bloomed in her chest. "He's going to talk to Maggie." Slade had only returned to Chicago yesterday.

Lucas tugged her attention to him. "Looks like we aren't the only ones about to start a new adventure."

Knowing that Slade and Maggie might work things out was the perfect ending to this day.

Lucas leaned down and kissed her. He was warm and familiar and absolutely wonderful. He tasted of sweet wine. Victoria couldn't wait to fill her days with gardening and cooking classes and middle-of-the-day lovemaking sessions with her hero.

Lucas drew back. "Wait right here."

Before Victoria could figure out what he had in mind, he had crossed the room and locked the door. Her jaw dropped when he strode back over to her and swept her into his arms.

"Lucas! What're you doing?" Her heart started that delicious pitter-patter.

He settled her on her private conference table, cleared the files aside with one sweep of his arm and proceeded to seduce her. She tried to keep her giggles quiet, but that was impossible with Lucas freeing her stockings from the lacy garters she bought just for him. He rolled off her stockings, slipped off her shoes and hiked the hem of her skirt up her thighs. The giggles quickly gave way to earthy moans and frantic touches.

She so loved this man.

Their adventures together were only beginning.

Chapter Twenty

Maggie's Coffee Shop, 6:30 p.m.

Where the heck was all her help tonight? Two people had called in sick.

Maggie rushed around behind the counter like a madwoman. Things hadn't been this busy this early on a Friday night in she didn't know when. She leaned against the counter a moment and swiped her brow with the back of her hand. In spite of the exhaustion, she smiled. Her hand flattened on her belly. The doctor had given her a clean bill of health. She was now on prenatal vitamins, and next month she would have her first ultrasound.

Her sisters were so happy for her. She felt amazing. Every day was a test of her self-discipline not to start shopping for the baby already. Her sisters advised her to wait at least until she knew if she was having a boy or a girl.

If only…

The bell over the door jingled. It was a miracle she heard it over the hum of conversation and TGIF laughter. Her gaze drifted to the door.

He walked in. As he had hundreds of times before.

But this time everything was different. There were no more secrets between them. Her heart leaped. Twelve whole days had passed since she'd seen or talked to him. He had explained about the work he had to do with the CIA in Mexico. And about burying his sister. And, truth was, they had both needed time and space to get their lives together.

With a quick glance at the crowd, he walked over to his seat. For the life of her she hadn't been able to let the servers start seating people in his spot. It was silly, she knew. But it just was.

The black trousers he wore fit his powerful body perfectly. The black sweater showcased that amazing torso. Heat rushed through her. God, she loved looking at him. She had missed him.

Maggie swiped her hands on her apron and walked around the bar. Her heart had already started its acrobatics. She strolled up to his table with as much non-chalance as she could muster and smiled. "Colombian dark roast?"

He smiled. A real, I'm-happy smile. She melted and he hadn't even spoken a word. "Actually, I need to speak to the owner."

Maggie tucked a handful of hair behind her ear and took a breath for courage. "I'm the owner." She thrust out her hand. "Maggie James."

He took her hand in his and gave it a squeeze. "Slade Keaton."

The crazy mixture of emotions that simple touch evoked had her trembling inside. "What can I do for you?"

He flared his hands. "I just got a new job." He hitched a thumb toward the street. "Over at the Colby Agency."

Maggie bit her lip and resisted the urge to jump up in the air and give a hoot. "You don't say."

"Thing is, I need a place to stay. I checked out a couple of places, but I need a woman's opinion."

Maggie was afraid to breathe. "Really? I suppose I can help you with that."

"Great." He stood and offered his hand. "You mind taking a ride with a guy you just met?"

"Technically we met two years ago," she countered.

"That was the old me. You've never met this me."

She put her hand in his and nodded. She couldn't speak. Not without breaking down.

THE DRIVE SEEMED TO TAKE forever. Slade wanted to push the accelerator through the floor, but he had to drive safely. He was carrying precious cargo. He hoped Maggie understood what he meant back at the coffee shop. He was a new man and he was giving it all he had. Slade wanted this to work more than he had ever wanted anything in his life.

He pulled into the driveway and shut off the engine.

Maggie leaned forward. "This is a house."

He shrugged. "Wait till you see the yard in the daylight."

She was out of the car before he'd finished the statement. He grinned. She liked it and they weren't even inside yet.

He watched her climb the two steps up to the broad front porch. The house was a Craftsman style. With a big backyard and an amazing front porch. Slade had had no idea what kind of house Maggie would like, so he'd done his research. He'd called her sisters. Two days of exchanging images and emails, another two days of waiting for a Realtor to find just the right house and he'd bought this one this morning.

Maggie peered through one of the front windows. "I wish it weren't so dark in there. I can't see a thing."

Slade walked straight up to the door and pulled out a key. He unlocked the door while she watched in amazement, and then he reached inside and flipped on a light.

Maggie stared from him to the open door and back. "How did you…?"

Slade scooped her into his arms and crossed the threshold. Her sister had told him to do that even though they weren't married yet. But that was next on his agenda. He and Maggie had done everything else backward, why not this?

When he settled her onto her feet, she wandered from room to room. The place was just what her sisters said she had always wanted. Lots of original detail. Shiny wooden floors that were original, too. And a kitchen that looked accurate to the period, but was actually filled with the latest technology.

By the time she'd seen the three bedrooms upstairs, she collapsed on the steps at the bottom of the staircase.

Slade sat down beside her. "You think this might work?"

Maggie swiped her cheeks.

"Are you crying?" But that was good, he thought.

She shook her head. "I'm fine."

He tilted her face up to his. "You are crying."

"It's just so beautiful." The tears fell in earnest now. "When I was a little girl I used to cut pictures from magazines and paste them into my dream book." She swiped her eyes again. "How could you possibly know?"

"Your sisters told me." In his whole life he had never

had anything give him more joy than this moment. Seeing her so happy made him happy.

"Okay." She took another of those deep breaths, then she turned those emerald eyes up to his. "Why did you rent the house of my dreams?" Her voice trembled.

Slade took her hand in his and tried to find a place to begin. "First, I didn't rent the house, I bought it." Her eyes grew rounder still. "I want our child to have a real home."

The tears started again. He wiped them away with the pads of his thumbs. "I don't know if I'll be any good at the father gig, but I want to try. I've already made an appointment with a psychologist that helped Jim out a few years ago. I want to fix me."

MAGGIE THREW HER ARMS around him and hugged him so tight. She didn't ever want to let go. She kissed him hard on the lips and then sat back. A couple of seconds were necessary to pull herself back together. There were things she had wanted to say to him for days. But he'd had a lot to take care of and she'd thrown herself into work to keep her mind occupied.

"First," she began as he had, "I am so proud of you. The amount of courage it takes to do what you're doing…" She shook her head when she couldn't find the words. Words felt inadequate right now. "Well, it just amazes me. I love you, Slade Keaton, for who you are, who you've been and who I know you'll be in the future. A wonderful father." She wanted to add *husband,* but they hadn't talked about that step yet. And that was okay with her. He needed time and she understood that.

"I appreciate the vote of confidence." He hesitated a moment before saying more, but she knew he had more to say. "You told me that you didn't want me back for the baby. You wanted me back if I wanted this relationship."

How selfish of her to have thrown those words at him. She hadn't known all that he'd suffered. "I didn't understand. I—"

He pressed his fingers to her lips. "You were right. This relationship has to be about all three of us. Not just one or two."

Maggie didn't know whether to cry or to shout for joy.

"It'll take time." He shrugged. "Maybe years. But I do know this." He took her hands in his and then he moved in front of her and got down on one knee. "If missing someone so badly that you can't eat or sleep is love… If feeling like that person is a part of you that you can't live without is love… If that person is the first thing on your mind in the morning and the last thing at night is love…then this has to be love."

Maggie couldn't keep the tears back. "Are you sure about this?"

He reached into his pocket and pulled out a ring. "Sure enough." He smiled as Maggie cried. "Maggie James, if I prove I can learn to be a good husband and father, will you be my wife?"

"Yes."

He kissed her. God, she had missed him. The way he looked, the way he talked and the way he kissed. Everything about him. She melted into the kiss, wanting it to go on forever. But he pulled back long enough to slide the ring onto her finger.

Maggie adored the ring. A beautiful princess-cut diamond. "When did you figure all this out?"

"I thought about Victoria and Lucas. Jim and Tasha. And half a dozen other couples from the Colby Agency. The idea has been in my head for a while. I knew what I wanted to do. It was only a matter of logistics. Mostly mine."

Maggie scrubbed the tears from her cheeks and looked around. "We have to go shopping." He looked confused. "We need furniture and stuff." The sudden change of subject was wacky, she knew, but she just couldn't absorb all this.

His expression brightened as if he'd just thought of something. "We have stuff."

Maggie frowned, confused. "Where?"

"Come on." He grabbed her hand and tugged her up the stairs.

"But we've already been up here." There was nothing up there.

He led her to the master bedroom before releasing her hand.

"Slade, what are you doing?" She shook her head as he ducked into the closet. What was he up to? Curious as she was, she couldn't wait to call her sisters. This was like a fairy tale come true. *Her* fairy tale.

Slade spread a blanket on the floor. Maggie started to tease him about what he obviously had on his mind, but he held up a finger for her to wait.

He went back to the closet and brought out a bottle of champagne, a tray and two delicate stemmed glasses. "Nonalcoholic," he said before placing the tray on the floor and arranging the bottle and glasses. He made another trip to the closet for a bowl of fruit and a small plate of cheese and crackers.

Maggie was exhausted just watching him. "This is too much, Slade. You didn't have to do all this."

Slade took her into his arms and lifted her against him. "Get used to it." He laid her on the blanket and stretched out next to her. "You saved me, Maggie."

She stroked his jaw. "You saved yourself. I just cheered you on."

"No," he insisted. "No one ever believed in me the way you do. You made me want to be the kind of man you deserve. You made me want to feel all the things I was trained not to feel."

Maggie pushed him onto his back and straddled his waist. "Good. Then feel this." She scooted down his legs and removed his shoes. Then she slithered back up to his waist and stripped off his trousers.

Slowly but surely she removed each item of clothing. When he was naked, she crawled up his body on all fours. She nipped at his rock-hard belly. "Feel that?"

"Oh, yeah."

She traced a path down his belly with her tongue. When her cheek brushed his arousal, she asked, "Feel that?"

He groaned an affirmative.

She went on that way until she had tasted all those sensitive erogenous zones. Then she taunted him with a little striptease. By the time she settled onto him, uniting their bodies completely, they were both ready to shatter.

Maggie lay in his arms afterward. She had missed him so badly. If she had her way, they would never be apart again.

"I was thinking," he said, his voice huskier than usual from their lovemaking.

She raised up, propped on his chest and smiled at him. "Yes?" She loved his voice. She would rather listen to him talk than to eat…most of the time. Lately, she'd been eating everything in sight.

"Thanksgiving is coming up. Maybe we can invite your family here. Show off the house."

Maggie's gaze narrowed. "My sisters put you up to that, didn't they?" She knew a lot could change in twelve days, but this was a little much.

Slade toyed with a strand of her hair. "It might have been suggested during the course of one of our conversations."

Uncontrollable laughter claimed her. Maggie's sisters had big bad Slade eating out of their hands. He tickled her. Kissed her neck and any other part of her that made her giggle.

Maggie dropped back on the blanket. She had to catch her breath. Lately she'd been sleeping like a rock at night. That happened in the first trimester, she'd learned. Speaking of sleep, she would miss her apartment. It was handy living right over the coffee shop. The commute to work every day from here would take some getting used to.

"Did I miss something?" He lay on his side, propped up on his elbow.

"What? No." She shook her head. "I was just thinking."

"About?"

"The apartment. The coffee shop."

He traced a finger down her rib cage. "The apartment would make a great perk for a manager."

Maggie smiled. She had been thinking the same

thing. "I'd have plenty of time to get things in order before the baby comes."

"Plenty."

Was she dreaming? Maggie resisted the impulse to pinch herself.

Slade leaned down and whispered against her belly.

Maggie stared down at him, puzzled but pleased.

He glanced up at her and smiled. "I'm talking to the baby."

That was the sweetest thing she had ever heard. "Did my sisters tell you to do that, too?"

"Nope." He kissed her tummy. "I bought a guide-book."

She ran her fingers through his silky hair and thanked God he had saved this man and brought him back to her. "Maybe I need to read that book."

He crawled up next to her and kissed her on the nose. "We'll read it together. And in a couple of years we'll make him or her a baby brother or sister."

"I love the way you lay out a plan, Keaton."

"Hang around and I'll teach you a few things."

Maggie planned on it. Forever was a long time, but that was about what she had in mind.

* * * * *

SUSPENSE

Heartstopping stories of intrigue and mystery—
where true love always triumphs.

 Harlequin®

INTRIGUE®

COMING NEXT MONTH
AVAILABLE DECEMBER 6, 2011

#1317 BABY BATTALION
Daddy Corps
Cassie Miles

#1318 DADDY BOMBSHELL
Situation: Christmas
Lisa Childs

#1319 DADE
The Lawmen of Silver Creek Ranch
Delores Fossen

#1320 TOP GUN GUARDIAN
Brothers in Arms
Carol Ericson

#1321 NANNY 911
The Precinct: SWAT
Julie Miller

#1322 BEAR CLAW BODYGUARD
Bear Claw Creek Crime Lab
Jessica Andersen

You can find more information on upcoming Harlequin® titles,
free excerpts and more at www.HarlequinInsideRomance.com.

HICNM1111

REQUEST YOUR FREE BOOKS!
2 FREE NOVELS PLUS 2 FREE GIFTS!

❖ Harlequin®

INTRIGUE®

BREATHTAKING ROMANTIC SUSPENSE

YES! Please send me 2 FREE Harlequin Intrigue® novels and my 2 FREE gifts (gifts are worth about $10). After receiving them, if I don't wish to receive any more books, I can return the shipping statement marked "cancel." If I don't cancel, I will receive 6 brand-new novels every month and be billed just $4.49 per book in the U.S. or $5.24 per book in Canada. That's a saving of at least 14% off the cover price! It's quite a bargain! Shipping and handling is just 50¢ per book in the U.S. and 75¢ per book in Canada.* I understand that accepting the 2 free books and gifts places me under no obligation to buy anything. I can always return a shipment and cancel at any time. Even if I never buy another book, the two free books and gifts are mine to keep forever.

182/382 HDN FEQ2

Name _____ (PLEASE PRINT)

Address _____ Apt. #

City _____ State/Prov. _____ Zip/Postal Code

Signature (if under 18, a parent or guardian must sign)

Mail to the **Reader Service:**
IN U.S.A.: P.O. Box 1867, Buffalo, NY 14240-1867
IN CANADA: P.O. Box 609, Fort Erie, Ontario L2A 5X3

Not valid for current subscribers to Harlequin Intrigue books.

**Are you a subscriber to Harlequin Intrigue books
and want to receive the larger-print edition?
Call 1-800-873-8635 or visit www.ReaderService.com.**

* Terms and prices subject to change without notice. Prices do not include applicable taxes. Sales tax applicable in N.Y. Canadian residents will be charged applicable taxes. Offer not valid in Quebec. This offer is limited to one order per household. All orders subject to credit approval. Credit or debit balances in a customer's account(s) may be offset by any other outstanding balance owed by or to the customer. Please allow 4 to 6 weeks for delivery. Offer available while quantities last.

Your Privacy—The Reader Service is committed to protecting your privacy. Our Privacy Policy is available online at www.ReaderService.com or upon request from the Reader Service.

We make a portion of our mailing list available to reputable third parties that offer products we believe may interest you. If you prefer that we not exchange your name with third parties, or if you wish to clarify or modify your communication preferences, please visit us at www.ReaderService.com/consumerschoice or write to us at Reader Service Preference Service, P.O. Box 9062, Buffalo, NY 14269. Include your complete name and address.

HI11B

*Lucy Flemming and Ross Mitchell shared a magical,
sexy Christmas weekend together six years ago.
This Christmas, history may repeat itself when they find
themselves stranded in a major snowstorm…
and alone at last.*

Read on for a sneak peek from
IT HAPPENED ONE CHRISTMAS
by Leslie Kelly.

Available December 2011, only from Harlequin® Blaze™.

EYEING THE GRAY, THICK SKY through the expansive wall of
windows, Lucy began to pack up her photography gear.
The Christmas party was winding down, only a dozen or so
people remaining on this floor, which had been transformed
from cubicles and meeting rooms to a holiday funland. She
smiled at those nearest to her, then, seeing the glances at her
silly elf hat, she reached up to tug it off her head.

Before she could do it, however, she heard a voice. A
deep, male voice—smooth and sexy, and so not Santa's.

"I appreciate you filling in on such short notice. I've
heard you do a terrific job."

Lucy didn't turn around, letting her brain process what
she was hearing. Her whole body had stiffened, the hairs on
the back of her neck standing up, her skin tightening into
tiny goose bumps. Because that voice sounded so familiar.
Impossibly familiar.

It can't be.

"It sounds like the kids had a great time."

Unable to stop herself, Lucy began to turn around,
wondering if her ears—and all her other senses—were
deceiving her. After all, six years was a long time, the mind

could play tricks. What were the odds that she'd bump into *him*, here? And today of all days. December 23.

Six years exactly. Was that really possible?

One look—and the accompanying frantic thudding of her heart—and she knew her ears and brain were working just fine. Because it was *him*.

"Oh, my God," he whispered, shocked, frozen, staring as thoroughly as she was. "Lucy?"

She nodded slowly, not taking her eyes off him, wondering why the years had made him even more attractive than ever. It didn't seem fair. Not when she'd spent the past six years thinking he must have started losing that thick, golden-brown hair, or added a spare tire to that trim, muscular form.

No.

The man was gorgeous. Truly, without-a-doubt, mouthwateringly handsome, every bit as hot as he'd been the first time she'd laid eyes on him. She'd been twenty-two, he one year older.

They'd shared an amazing holiday season.

And had never seen one another again.

Until now.

Find out what happens in
IT HAPPENED ONE CHRISTMAS
by Leslie Kelly.
Available December 2011, only from Harlequin® Blaze™

HBEXP1211

Harlequin®

ROMANTIC
SUSPENSE

USA TODAY BESTSELLING AUTHOR

MARIE FERRARELLA

Brings you another exciting installment from

CAVANAUGH
JUSTICE

A Cavanaugh Christmas

When Detective Kaitlyn Two Feathers follows a kidnapping case outside her jurisdiction, she enlists the aid of Detective Thomas Cavelli. Still reeling from the discovery that his father was a Cavanaugh, Thomas takes the case, thinking it will be a nice distraction...until Kaitlyn becomes his ultimate distraction. As the case heats up and time is running out, Thomas must prove to Kaitlyn that he is trustworthy and risk it all for the one thing they both never thought they'd find—love.

Available November 22 wherever books are sold!

www.Harlequin.com

HRS27753